CHINON, FRANCE, 1942

I was thirteen years old in October, 1942, when my best friend, Emile Levy, was put into a cattle truck along with the rest of his family, and taken by train to an unknown destination. It was only after the War was over we learned that Emile's family and other Jews were sent to an extermination camp in Poland called Auschwitz where they were murdered in their millions. It was after Emile was taken away that I became involved with the Resistance against the German occupation of my country. This is my story.

MAY 1943

My name is Paul Lelaud. I am 13 years and 11 months old. I live with my mother and her brother, Uncle Maurice, in rooms above his bakery shop in Chinon, a small town on the banks of the River Vienne in France. My father, Albert, was killed fighting the Germans when they invaded France three years ago.

My mother has a photograph of my father on the sideboard in the small house we share with Uncle Maurice. He is dressed very smartly, in a suit and wearing a shirt with a big tie, and holding a hat in his hand. But I remember my father very differently. Before he joined the Army and went to war, my father was a driver, carrying goods on his horse-driven cart from town to town in the Loire Valley where we lived. I remember the way he smelled – of straw and horses. If the load was very heavy, my father would use two horses to pull his cart along the rutted road. Otherwise, he would use one of the horses and leave the other to rest. He would then work that horse the next day while the other rested. My father was a very fair man and very kind to his horses, and to me and my mother. He used to laugh a lot and sing songs to us.

I remember the day the Germans invaded. It was 10 May 1940. German troops and tanks came across the border into the north of France. Everyone had been expecting an attack like this for years, ever since the Great War ended in 1918, so the Government had begun to build a wall between France and Germany. It was called the Maginot Line and it was supposed to be a defence that no invading army could break through. It had anti-tank defences all the way along it, was made of concrete and steel and was bomb-proof, and every 100 yards or so there was a pillbox, a small concrete building with machine guns poking out of a little slit. My father, who had joined the Army when war broke out the year before, was stationed at the northern end of the Maginot Line, where it was still being built.

The Germans didn't break through the Maginot Line, instead they went round it, and then they attacked the French troops at each end of it from behind.

We heard the news on the radio, and then read about it in the newspapers. No one really believed it. People in our town said the French Army would fight back, and with the help of the British and the Belgians we would push the Germans back out of France. In the event, it happened quite differently. The Germans pushed forward faster. The Belgians surrendered. The British Army was forced back to Dunkirk, a town on the coast off the English Channel, and was taken back to England by hundreds of small boats.

All the time I kept waiting for my father to come home so I could ask him what had really happened. What had he seen? What had the battle been like? But there was no word from him – no letters, not even a postcard.

And then the postman came with a letter from the Ministry of Defence. It was addressed to my mother. It said that my father had been killed fighting to defend his country.

At first I couldn't believe it. I was sure it was a mistake and that my father would arrive at the door of our small house in the centre of Chinon with a big smile and an even bigger hug for me and my mother, and a cheery wave for Uncle Maurice. But it didn't happen. My father was dead – murdered by the Germans.

My mother cried for the whole of that first day. No one could comfort her. She went upstairs to the room they shared, clutching the letter in her hand, and lay on their big wooden bed and sobbed.

Uncle Maurice didn't know how to handle her. He had never been married himself as far as I knew. At first, while she lay upstairs and cried, he tried to ignore her. Then, as her crying got louder and turned into a wild howling, he became embarrassed and went up to the room and banged on the door and said, "Angeline, quieten down, the neighbours will hear."

She quietened down a bit, but not for long, and we spent the rest of that day in the kitchen at the back of my uncle's bakery, trying to pretend that we couldn't hear my mother's pitiful wailing.

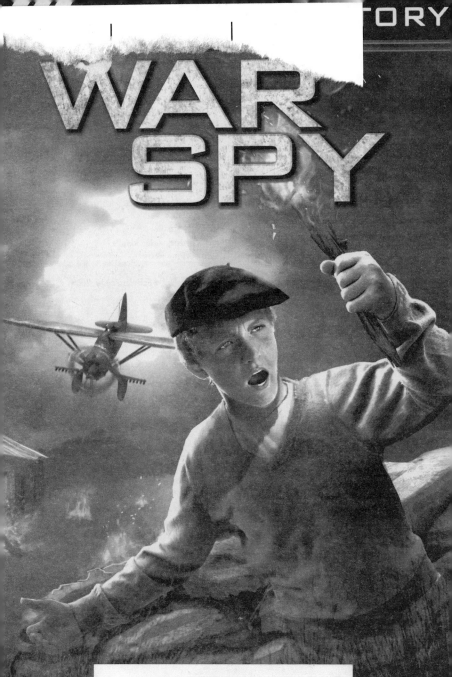

WAR SPY

To Lynne, with love

While the events described and some of the characters in this book may be based on actual historical events and real people, Paul Lelaud is a fictional character, created by the author, and his story is a work of fiction.

Scholastic Children's Books
Commonwealth House, 1–19 New Oxford Street,
London, WC1A 1NU, UK
A division of Scholastic Ltd
London ~ New York ~ Toronto ~ Sydney ~ Auckland
Mexico City ~ New Delhi ~ Hong Kong

First published in the UK as *My Story: Spy Smuggler* by Scholastic Ltd, 2004
This edition published 2013

Printed and bound in the UK by CPI Group (UK) Ltd, Croydon, CR0 4YY

2 4 6 8 10 9 7 5 3 1

The right of Jim Eldridge to be identified as the author of this work has been asserted by him in accordance with the Copyright, Designs and Patents Act, 1988.

I wanted to cry, but I didn't want to do it in public, with everyone watching and listening. I kept my tears for the privacy of my own room that night, when I thought of my father, and the fact that he would never take me for a ride on his horse and cart ever again, or play with me, or take me walking with him. His death had left a hole in my heart and in my life that I knew I could never fill.

After they had invaded, the Germans kept advancing and the French Army kept retreating south. Those soldiers who didn't retreat were either killed or taken prisoner and sent to camps in Germany.

A month later, on Wednesday, 19 June 1940, it was my eleventh birthday. It was also the day the German troops – hundreds of them, with tanks and huge guns on wheels – arrived within sight of Chinon. A troop of French soldiers had come into the town to defend it the week before. Many of the townspeople were terrified that if our soldiers fought back the Germans would start shelling the town. So my Uncle Maurice and some of the other shopkeepers went to see the Mayor of Chinon, Monsieur Mattraits, and begged him to surrender the town to the Germans. I only found out what Uncle Maurice had done when he came back from seeing the Mayor and told my mother about the meeting. We were in the small kitchen at the back of his shop. I was so angry with him I nearly burst into tears with anger.

"We must never surrender!" I shouted.

Uncle Maurice took off his jacket and tie and hung them on a hook on the back of the door.

"You don't understand, Paul," he said.

"The Germans killed my father!" I spat at him.

"And they will kill you, too, and all the rest of us if we resist them," said Uncle Maurice.

"I don't care!" I shouted at him. "You are a coward! All the people in this town are cowards if they surrender to the Germans!"

Uncle Maurice went white and he glared at me, his face grim. Then he turned to my mother.

"I will not be called a coward in my own home", he said. "Even though you are my sister, Angeline, if you do not keep that son of yours under control, I will put both of you out on the street."

With that, Uncle Maurice left the kitchen and went into his shop.

My mother turned to me, and there were tears in her eyes.

"I know you are angry, Paul," she said, "and believe me, I miss your father more than I can say, but these are difficult times. Your uncle is only doing what he thinks is best for all of us and we cannot afford for him to turn us out of this house. There is nowhere else for us to go. Please, I beg you, Paul, keep your feelings to yourself. Until this is all over."

I looked at the photograph of my father on the sideboard,

at his big smile, his kindly eyes, and I wanted to shout out, "No, I won't! I'm going to tell everyone how I feel! I hate the Germans! We should all rise up and fight them. And if they kill us all, then so be it! I would rather die than live as a slave of the Germans!" But then I looked back at my mother, at the tears she was fighting back, and thought of her lying dead, killed by German shells or by bullets from a German fighter plane. My heart sank, and I nodded, though I could feel the tears coming into my own eyes. They were not just tears of sadness, but tears of frustration and bitterness and anger.

My mother came over to me and took me in her arms, almost smothering me.

"Thank you, Paul," she said, and now she began to cry in earnest. "I could not bear to lose you as well. We must stay alive at all costs. While we are alive, there is hope that we can fight the Germans and be free of them. If we are all dead, there will be no hope at all."

The next day the French soldiers left the town and retreated south. The day after that the German tanks rolled across the bridge over the River Vienne and into Chinon. Our freedom was at an end.

It was the day before my fourteenth birthday. As I was about to cycle to school I discovered my bicycle had a puncture. Because I didn't have time to repair it, I decided to walk the two miles to school. As I walked, I realized bitterly that it was three years since the Germans invaded our town, and they were showing no signs of leaving. For three years we had lived under German occupation, with their tanks and armed soldiers in our streets, and all the best food going to feed them. In those three years there had been many bombing raids by Allied planes to try to drive the Germans out, but all that happened was that French towns were destroyed and French people killed by the bombing. The Germans kept themselves safe underground.

As I walked to school I thought of our teacher, Monsieur Armignac, and how much I hated him. Monsieur Armignac had photographs of Adolf Hitler and our Head of State, Marshal Pétain, on the walls of our classroom, and we were expected to salute both pictures every morning. If we didn't, we got six strokes of the cane on our hands and Monsieur Armignac would threaten to tell the Germans that we were traitors, and say that our parents would be arrested and sent to work in the labour camps in Germany.

To avoid getting beaten by him, we all saluted the pictures but I kept the fingers of my other hand crossed, so it didn't really count. We used to laugh at Monsieur Armignac behind his back about this, that is, until my best friend Emile Levy and his family were taken away.

Emile was a Jew. I never knew why Hitler and the Germans, and French people like Monsieur Armignac hated Jews. I remember Emile saying to me: "My father says some people just hate Jews because it's easy to hate people who are different."

Emile and I had been standing in the school playground with our friends the Marchand brothers, Antoine, Denis and Jean. They lived on a farm just outside Chinon and came to school every day on their father's cart.

"But you're not different," I protested. "You're the same as us. You look the same as us."

"Except Emile's got dark hair and my hair is red," said Denis. "And Antoine's is a sort of brown, and Jean's is yellow. And Paul's is a sort of grey colour."

"That's because of all the flour he gets on his head from working at his uncle's bakery," laughed Jean.

"I heard the priest, Father Metier, and Monsieur Armignac talking, and Father Metier said the Jews killed Jesus," said Antoine. Denis looked puzzled.

"I thought Jesus was a Jew," he said. "There was that thing about him being King of the Jews."

"I know," said Jean with a sigh. "It doesn't make sense. Jesus' mother and father, Mary and Joseph, were Jews. So surely he was one as well?"

We all agreed this was too difficult for us to understand, and we also agreed that we all hated Hitler, the Germans, and Monsieur Armignac.

That conversation had been a long time ago. Before Emile had disappeared. My head was full of these thoughts when I heard my name being called from behind me. I looked round and saw Monsieur Marchand at the reins of his cart. Antoine, Denis and Jean were in the back, sitting on bales of straw.

"Come on, Paul, jump up!" called Monsieur Marchand.

I clambered up into the cart and joined the three brothers.

"Walk on!" Monsieur Marchand said clicking his tongue, and the cart began to roll forward.

"You're going to be fourteen tomorrow, Paul," said Denis. "You'll be able to leave school."

"I can't wait," I said. "The sooner I can get away from Monsieur Armignac, the better."

"What will you do?" asked Antoine. "Work for your uncle?"

I nodded. "I'd rather do that than work in a factory making guns and planes for the Germans," I said.

The others chorused in agreement.

"I'm going to work with Dad on the farm when I leave," said Antoine. He was the eldest of the three brothers and would be fourteen in July.

Denis was twelve and Jean was ten, so they both had a long time to stay at school before they could leave. I hoped for their sakes that the War ended soon and Monsieur Armignac was arrested and sent to prison for being a traitor to France. For anyone to suffer another four years of him was too horrible to even think about.

"I was just thinking about Emile," I said. "And that time we talked about him and his family being Jewish."

An awkward silence fell over the cart. Then Jean said, "I thought that Emile would have written to us. It's been eight months since he went away. He said he'd write."

"Maybe they're not allowed to write letters home when they're in the labour camp," said Denis. "Madame Bettinger said it's like being in prison. The guards watch them all the time."

"How does she know?" I asked.

"Madame Bettinger has a nephew who was in the Army. He was taken prisoner and sent to a labour camp. They let him come home last month."

"Perhaps they'll let Emile and his family come home," said Jean, hopefully.

Antoine and I exchanged brief glances, but said nothing to his two younger brothers. One day after school last October,

Antoine, Emile and I had been cycling home from school when we saw some German soldiers standing outside Emile's house. Emile's mother was in the doorway, pleading desperately with the soldiers, but their faces looked set and grim.

The three of us pulled up on our bikes and went to walk towards Madame Levy, but two of the soldiers stepped in front of us.

"Go away, this is none of your business!" snapped one of the soldiers.

"It is my business!" retorted Emile angrily. "This is my family!"

"Then you have one hour to get packed," snapped the soldier.

"They say they're putting us on a train and taking us away!" sobbed Madame Levy.

"Where to?" I asked.

"Do you two live here as well?" the soldier demanded of myself and Antoine.

"No," I said.

"Then get away from here!" he barked.

My head was in a whirl. What was going on?

"You'd better go," muttered Emile. "No sense in all three of us getting into trouble."

Two of the German soldiers hustled Emile and his mother in through their front door, and the one who had snapped at us now levelled his rifle at us.

"Go on!" he shouted. "I told you to go!"

Antoine and I hesitated. The German soldier jerked the barrel of his rifle so it was aiming straight at me.

"All right!" I said, angrily. "We're going!"

I took one last look at the house, but Emile was inside.

As Antoine and I rode away on our bicycles, Antoine said: "Let's sneak down to the railway station later. We might be able to see Emile then and say goodbye, before he goes."

I agreed. And so, that night, as dusk was falling, I set off for the railway station. I'd only been able to get out of the house because I'd told Uncle Maurice and my mother that I was going on my bike to see Antoine on the farm, and Antoine had told his parents that he was coming to see me.

We cycled to the station but we couldn't get near it because of the German troops, who had made a road block. They had rifles and they told us to turn around and go home.

"But we've come to see a friend of ours," said Antoine.

The German soldier laughed.

"There are no friends of yours here," he said. "Only Jews being taken away."

I saw that Antoine was going to say something else, but I pushed my bicycle so it knocked against him to shut him up, and then said, "Thank you. We'll go."

Antoine looked at me in surprise but then he saw my face and cycled away from the station in silence. We only went a little way, until we'd turned a bend in the road and were out of sight of the Germans, and then I stopped. Antoine stopped as well.

"What was all that about?" he asked indignantly. "Knocking me with your bike like that?"

"The road block. The way that soldier was standing, with his rifle ready. And the other soldiers behind him, all with rifles ready. This isn't just an ordinary train journey that Emile and his family are going on. Something's happening, and I want to find out what."

Antoine thought about this and then nodded.

"OK," he said.

We left our bikes in a small wood, hidden under some leaves, and then began to work our way through the trees towards the railway tracks.

We crept forward as far as we could without being seen, and then settled down into a hiding place behind some bushes, not far from the station.

It looked eerie. Instead of the usual lamps, the Germans had set up searchlights so that the platform was completely lit up. I could see Emile and his parents and his young sister standing on the platform, with their suitcases and bags beside them. Next to them was another family, Mr and Mrs Berg with their four children. They also had their bags piled up beside them.

Armed German soldiers stood on the platform close to them. I counted six soldiers, which seemed a lot just to look after four adults and six children. More armed soldiers marched up and down on the platforms. Then we heard the sound of the train approaching, the clank of its wheels and the hissing of steam from its engine, and the added hiss and squeal of the brakes as it neared the platform.

"What's going on?" whispered Antoine, puzzled. "That's not a proper train, it's a cattle truck."

Antoine was right. Instead of the usual carriages, the engine was hauling a series of cattle trucks, their big wooden doors firmly shut.

"It can't be for Emile and the others," said Antoine. "They must be bringing cattle to feed the Germans."

But when the train stopped and the doors of one of the trucks opened, we saw that there weren't cattle inside, but people. The German soldiers gestured at the open doors of the truck, urging the Levys and the Bergs to get on board. I could see Emile's father protesting. The Germans didn't bother to argue. One of the soldiers simply hit Mr Levy in the stomach with the barrel of his rifle. Mr Levy fell down, clutching his stomach. Then two more of the soldiers picked him up off the ground and dragged him to the open door of the cattle truck. They were just about to throw him in when there was a sudden commotion, and then we saw a woman run out of the truck. She pushed one of the German soldiers and he fell over, and the next minute the woman was running along the platform. And she was really running, not just little wobbly steps but hard running, like when someone is determined to win a race at all costs.

The German soldiers beside the cattle truck shouted at her to stop, but she kept running. I saw one of them raise his rifle to his shoulder and take aim at her, but before he could fire she had jumped down off the platform between the cattle trucks, and then she was out of our sight.

There was a lot of shouting from the soldiers by the cattle truck, followed by more shouting from the other soldiers at different points around the station.

"There she is!" whispered Antoine excitedly.

I followed his pointing finger, and saw her. The woman had come from behind the cattle trucks and was running along the railway track, stumbling a bit as she ran, but definitely putting distance between herself and the train.

A shot rang out, and the woman dropped. For a moment I thought she'd been hit, but I heard the bullet ricochet off a metal post near her. Then she got up and started running again.

"She's going to do it!" said Antoine. "She's getting away!"

And then a machine gun at the end of one of the platforms opened up, its bullets smashing and tearing into the ground near the woman, making it leap up around her as if it was exploding. And then she fell backwards, her arms outstretched. I could tell from the way she lay that she was dead.

Back on the platform, the soldiers were pushing Emile and his family and the Bergs into the truck. The last I saw of my friend was him dragging the family's big suitcase into the truck, then the huge wooden doors sliding shut behind him, bolted from the outside.

A guard blew a whistle and the train began to move.

A party of German soldiers walked along the track next to the train, heading towards the dead body of the woman.

"I don't want to stay here any more," I said.

I felt as if I was going to be sick, and I didn't want to be caught by the Germans.

Antoine, whose face was deathly pale, nodded, and we crept back to where we had hidden our bikes.

"What's going to happen to Emile?" asked Antoine, his voice shaking. "I don't know," I said, breathing hard with the shock.

"I think we ought to keep what we saw a secret," said Antoine. "I don't like to, but if we tell anyone and they tell the Germans, they'll come looking for us to shut us up. And that means they might take our families away, like Emile's."

I thought about this. I didn't want to keep it a secret, I wanted to tell everyone what the Germans had done that night: how they'd packed Emile and his family and the Bergs into trucks like cattle, and how they'd shot the woman. I wanted to make everyone so angry that they'd rise up against the Germans and throw them out of Chinon, out of France.

But I knew that they wouldn't. People were too scared of what the Germans would do. People like my Uncle Maurice would blame the woman who'd died, or Emile and his family, for causing trouble by stirring things up. And there were too many people like Monsieur Armignac, who supported the Germans and would back them up in whatever they did. Antoine was right – to protect our families, we had to keep what had happened at the station a secret. And so we did.

But Antoine and I were determined that the Germans wouldn't think we were all like Monsieur Armignac, so one night Antoine took a pot of paint and two brushes from his father's barn, and he and I painted the words "Free France" and "Death to Germans" on a wall in a part of the town where the Germans didn't patrol much.

We caused a great storm in Chinon. The German Commandant, General Fleischer, issued an order that anyone caught painting anti-German slogans would be arrested and sent to a labour camp. Some people told my mother that some young people had been caught painting anti-German slogans on walls in other towns, and they hadn't been sent to a labour camp but had been shot. Antoine and I decided that we'd stop painting the slogans, but we'd try and think up other ways we could let the Germans know how much true French people hated them.

I often thought about trying to find out where the Resistance was – the secret organization of French people that attacked Germans and cut their telephone lines and sabotaged their goods trains. I could volunteer to join them. But there was no Resistance in Chinon, just people who let the Germans walk all over them. It was a sickening and shameful time to be French.

As I stood behind my desk at school on that July morning, watching the sunshine coming in through the windows, I remembered that night last October, the last time I'd seen Emile, and once more I felt how much I hated living in my own country under German rule. School this day was as bad as ever, with Monsieur Armignac forcing us to stand and give the Nazi salute at the pictures of Adolf Hitler and Marshal Pétain at the start of the day, as usual.

I cheered up a bit at the thought that tomorrow I would be fourteen and would be able to leave school. I wouldn't have to put up with the shame of saluting the man who'd had my father killed, had Emile and his family taken away in a cattle truck, and the woman at the railway station mown down by a machine gun. In my eyes Marshal Pétain was just as bad as Hitler. Pétain was supposed to be the Head of the French State, but he wasn't really, and every true French person knew that. It had been the Germans who had made Pétain Head of State, with a government made up of people who supported Hitler and his Nazis. This so-called government wasn't even in Paris, the capital of France, but in a small town called Vichy. As far as I was concerned all of them were traitors to France. The true President of France was a man named Charles de Gaulle and he had been driven out of the country by the Germans when they invaded. For all these years de Gaulle had been working with the British to build up an army to attack France and drive the Germans out of our country.

After we'd saluted and said morning prayers, Monsieur Armignac ordered us to sit down, and then began to talk to us about how lucky we were to live in Chinon, under the protection of the German troops.

"In some other parts of France, people are in fear of their lives because of attacks by renegades and communists. It is important that we work together to keep our country safe from these traitors."

You're the traitor, Monsieur Armignac, I thought to myself, but I didn't look at him in case he saw what I was thinking. It would only give him a chance to beat me with his cane.

"Soon it will be the end of school for some of you," he continued. "You will be going out into the world. And, when you do, I want you to ask yourselves: 'What can I do for France? How can I help my country?' And the answer is, by helping our allies, the German people and their leader, Adolf Hitler. Because of the British and Americans and the Russians, this war grinds on. The sooner it can be brought to an end, the better it will be for everyone. But for that to happen, our allies need our help. They need labour. They need soldiers. I urge all you boys who are leaving school to join with our friends in the glorious German Army."

"Never!" shouted a voice, and then I realized with horror that the voice was mine. Although I had promised my mother and my uncle that I wouldn't get into trouble at school, or upset Monsieur Armignac, I couldn't help myself.

I saw Antoine looking at me, his mouth open in shock, and the next second there was the thwack! of Monsieur Armignac's cane smashing down on the desk in front of me.

"You dare to say such a thing, Lelaud!" raged Monsieur Armignac, his voice quivering with anger.

"Yes, I do!" I shouted back. "The Germans killed my father. They killed many French people, not just in this war but in the last…!"

"Silence!" stormed Monsieur Armignac. "I will not tolerate this … treasonable talk! Stand up at once and hold out your hand!"

I knew this meant he was going to cane me, at least six strokes across each hand, but I was so angry that I wasn't going to stand for it.

"No!" I snapped back curtly. "Tomorrow I am fourteen and I'll be old enough to leave this school, and you'll have no more power over me! But I refuse to be beaten by you on this last day."

"Refuse, do you?" roared Monsieur Armignac, and the next second there was a pain like sudden fire across my face as he hit me with his cane. Tears sprang into my eyes, and then his cane lashed down on me again, this time on the top of my head.

I was in such rage and pain that I didn't know what I was doing, I just knew that I wasn't going to let him carry on beating me like that. I found myself hitting out and kicking, both hands and feet swinging and striking out. I heard screams from the other children, and gasps from Monsieur Armignac as he collapsed to the floor.

I fell on top of him, just as if it had been a fight in the playground, and started punching him. Then I felt myself being dragged off him.

"Stop, Paul!" shouted a voice.

It was Antoine. He and Denis and Jean were holding me back, away from the figure of my teacher on the floor. Monsieur Armignac squirmed, putting his hand to his nose. Blood oozed out from between his fingers.

"You've done it now!" exclaimed Antoine in a voice filled with horror.

I looked down at Monsieur Armignac as he struggled to sit up, and then I pulled free of Antoine and the other boys, and ran for the door. Whatever else happened to me, I was finished with school, and school was finished with me.

I ran all the way home. When I got there, only my mother was in.

"Paul," she said, surprised. "You're home from school early. Is anything wrong?" Then she saw the lash mark across my face from where Monsieur Armignac had hit me with his cane, and her hand went to her mouth in horror. "Paul? What has happened?" she asked.

"Nothing," I said, breathlessly. "I tripped and fell and caught myself on a desk. Monsieur Armignac said I could go home, in case I had hit my head. Where's Uncle Maurice?" I asked, to divert her attention away from me.

"He's out delivering bread," she said. She looked at me closer, raising one of my eyelids to look into my eye. "Are you sure you're all right?" she asked.

"Yes," I said. "But my head hurts a bit. I think I'll just go and lie down."

With that I hurried upstairs to my room.

I had only been there for about half an hour, when I heard the sound of heavy boots in the bakery shop below, and the muffled sound of someone saying my name.

I got up and looked out of the window. There was nothing to be seen in the street.

Cautiously, I came out of my room and began to creep downstairs.

"Paul, is that you?" came my mother's voice from the shop.

"Yes, Mother," I replied walking into the shop.

The local police sergeant, Sergeant Boulet, was standing with a party of four German soldiers, all very grim-faced and all of them armed. Sergeant Boulet looked very unhappy. He glanced at me, sighed deeply, then turned grimly back to my mother.

"I am sorry, Angeline," he told her, "but I am here to arrest your son Paul."

For a moment I thought mother was going to faint.

"Paul?" she repeated dumbly. "On what charge? What do they think he has done?"

"He attacked Monsieur Armignac at school and beat him badly," replied Boulet.

Mother turned to me, an expression of sheer horror on her face.

"Paul," she begged, "tell them you didn't do it. Tell them this is a mistake."

I lowered my head.

"I'm sorry, mother," I said. "I did hit Monsieur Armignac, but only because he hit me."

Mother stared at me, her face growing whiter as the blood drained out of it. Sergeant Boulet gave an awkward cough.

"We have to take him with us, Angeline," he said uncomfortably.

Mother looked at the four German soldiers, standing stiffly to attention, their rifles held ready.

"No!" she begged. "They cannot shoot him! All he did was hit someone. A piece of temper, that's all it was. He didn't mean any harm! Please, Gerard…"

"These soldiers are not here to shoot him, Angeline, they are here to help me carry out my duty. You know the rules, if a violent criminal is to be arrested—"

"But Paul is not violent!" protested mother.

"I'm sorry, Angeline," said Sergeant Boulet. "I have my duty to perform. Paul has to come with me."

"Where?"

"To the police station. Monsieur Armignac has laid a complaint against him, and I have to keep him in a cell under lock and key while it is decided what to do with him."

"What do you mean, 'what to do with him'?" demanded my mother.

By now she was almost hysterical but she was playing for time – if she kept talking and asking questions then they wouldn't take me away.

"That will be up to the magistrate, and the Commandant," answered Boulet. Then he lowered his voice and appealed to my mother: "Please, Angeline, he must come with us, otherwise I shall have to arrest you all. I promise you, while he is under my care at the police station, he will be looked after."

By whom? I thought sourly. By German soldiers who'd come into my cell and kick me and beat me? Or who'd hold me while Monsieur Armignac beat me? For a moment I thought about slamming the door shut in their faces and running through the house and out of the back door, but then the image of the woman I'd seen shot at the railway station came into my mind. If I ran, that's what would happen to me. And, if Mother tried to intervene, she'd be shot as well. There was no escape for me.

"I shall be all right, Mother," I said, trying to appear calm and strong for her sake.

And with that Sergeant Boulet marched me off to the police station, the four German soldiers accompanying us, two on either side. Behind me I heard my mother begin to cry, and it tore at my heart to hear it. But I gritted my teeth and walked on, the tramp tramp tramp of the soldier's feet drilling into my brain as the metal-shod heels of their boots rang on the cobbles. My mother's cries grew louder and louder, but I didn't look back.

My first day in the cell at the police station was one of the most terrifying days of my life. I spent the whole time sitting on the hard bunk-bed, or pacing around the tiny room, dreading that any moment the door would open and the Germans would take me out and shoot me. Instead, after Sergeant Boulet had put me in the cell, he came back every so often to make sure that I was comfortable, and to ask me if I needed anything to read to pass the time. The trouble was, every time he unlocked the cell door to see if I was all right, I thought it was the Germans coming for me, and I had to fight to stop myself from visibly trembling with fear.

By the time evening came, and Sergeant Boulet bought me something to eat, there had still been no sign of my enemy.

"When will the Germans be coming for me?" I asked.

"I hope the Germans won't be coming for you at all," replied Sergeant Boulet.

"But I attacked Monsieur Armignac," I said.

"Your attack on Monsieur Armignac was a criminal offence," explained Sergeant Boulet. "It's for the magistrate to decide what to do with you."

Even though he said this, I thought it was only to make me feel better. Monsieur Armignac was the Germans' greatest friend in Chinon. I was sure they would see an attack on him as an attack on them.

When darkness came I thought I wouldn't be able to sleep for worrying about what was going to happen to me, but the events of the day had left me exhausted and I slept soundly until Sergeant Boulet woke me the next morning with a breakfast of a roll and a cup of coffee.

My mother came to see me early in the morning. Sergeant Boulet put me in a small room with her, the "visitors room", for about ten minutes. It seemed a very long time. Mother didn't say much, she cried a lot and worried about what was going to happen to me. For her sake, I had to hide the fear that I felt and pretend that everything was all right, and that I wasn't really worried. But the truth was, I was scared stiff. In fact for the whole of the first week, I remained terrified. Despite what Sergeant Boulet had said about the Germans not being involved, I didn't believe him. The Germans were involved in everything that went on in France. I stayed in the cell in the police station for two weeks. Every day I woke up on the hard narrow bed expecting to be taken to court and put up before the magistrate, or – even worse – to be taken to the German Commander's HQ, interrogated, tortured, and then shot. Instead, the same thing happened every day. Sergeant Boulet, or one of the other officers, brought me a roll and coffee for breakfast. I emptied my toilet bucket, washed, and then went back to the cell and sat on the bed. The barred window was too high up the wall for me to be able to see out of, so I contented myself with walking backwards and forwards across the cell for exercise.

Although Sergeant Boulet sometimes brought in newspapers and magazines for me to read, during those two weeks I had little else to do but sit alone and think about my life, and France under the Germans. I thought of how unfair it was that a good man like my father should be dead, and an evil hateful man like Monsieur Armignac should prosper. I thought of the woman that Antoine and I had seen shot at the railway station. And I thought of Emile, and wondered how he was. Where was he? How were the Germans treating him? If the cattle truck they'd taken Emile and his family away in was anything to go by, then I guessed they were having a pretty rough time of it. Most of the time, I wondered if I'd ever see Emile again.

For the whole two weeks, my mother came to see me every day, and every day she cried as soon as she saw me.

"Please, Mother, don't cry all the time," I begged her. "Sergeant Boulet has been as good as his word. I am safe and well here. It's boring, but I can live with that."

"But what will happen to you?" cried my mother.

The trouble was, I didn't know.

Then, one day early in July, Sergeant Boulet opened the

door of my cell and stepped to one side. He said, "You're free to go, Paul."

Free? I looked at him, puzzled.

"But the charges…?" I began.

"Monsieur Armignac has dropped the charges against you," said Boulet. "Your Uncle Maurice has come to take you home."

I followed Sergeant Boulet to the reception desk by the entrance to the police station. It felt good to be able to walk a distance after all this time, but I didn't feel good about facing Uncle Maurice.

Uncle Maurice didn't speak when I appeared, he just stood and scowled at me as Sergeant Boulet filled out the forms to have me released. This was the first time I had seen Uncle Maurice since I had been arrested. He obviously hadn't cared enough about me to come and visit me. Or perhaps he was just scared of being associated with someone who had attacked the Germans' favourite schoolmaster.

I followed Uncle Maurice out of the police station, and we set off on the walk home. So far we hadn't even said hello to one another.

"Thank you for coming to collect me," I said.

Uncle Maurice just grunted and shrugged, and we walked on.

It was still early in the morning and the streets of Chinon were quiet. A German patrol approached us, and Uncle

Maurice nodded to them in greeting. I felt anger rising inside me. Why did he treat them as if they were our friends? They were our enemies! I turned my head away from the patrol as they passed us.

We walked a bit more in silence, and then I blurted out, "Why did Monsieur Armignac drop the charges?"

"Because I paid him off," said Uncle Maurice.

I looked at my uncle, stunned.

"What?" I stammered.

"The time in jail hasn't improved your hearing, then," snapped Maurice. "I said I paid him off. It cost five hundred francs."

"Five hundred…?" I echoed, my mouth opening and closing in astonishment. I didn't realize that Uncle Maurice had 50 francs, let alone 500.

"Will you stop repeating everything I say!" snapped Maurice. "It was either that or have to live with my sister filling the house with weeping the whole time."

"Thank you, Uncle, but there was no need," I said stiffly. The thought of Monsieur Armignac getting 500 francs as a reward for beating me made me feel sick. "I would have been happy to serve my sentence."

"What sentence?" said Maurice angrily. "They would have shot you, you idiot!"

"Shot me?" I queried, stunned. "Just for attacking Monsieur Armignac?"

"Monsieur Armignac is a figurehead for those French people who support the Nazis," said Maurice. "An attack on him is seen as an attack on the Nazis. And your age is no excuse. If it had come to court, the sentence would have been death."

"I would have been happy to die as an example to the rest of France."

"Will you shut up about dying," said Maurice. "This country doesn't need more dead heroes, it needs living people prepared to fight for it."

"By baking bread for the Germans?" I jeered at him.

Even as I said it, I wished I hadn't. Whatever I thought about him, Uncle Maurice had managed to raise 500 francs to buy my freedom. He had bought my life. And this was how I paid him back – by sneering at him. He may not be a hero like my father had been, fighting against the Germans as a soldier, but he wasn't like Monsieur Armignac. There were no pictures of Adolf Hitler in our house.

"I am sorry, Uncle," I mumbled shamefaced. "That was unfair of me."

Uncle Maurice didn't say anything. We walked in an awkward silence for a few minutes, and then I tried to apologize again.

"I really am sorry." I said. "Someone has to bake bread, and if the Germans…"

"Shut up!" Uncle Maurice thundered.

I shut up.

"I've had a word with some friends," said Maurice, "and we all agree that the way you're going about things, you're a danger. And not just to yourself. A loose cannon like you can mess lots of things up. So we've decided to bring you in."

I looked at him, puzzled.

"Bring me in? Bring me in to what?" I asked.

"You'll find out later this afternoon," he said.

"Why later?" I asked. "Why not now?"

"Because you'll mess things up."

"How can I mess things up if I don't know what they are?" I demanded, frustrated.

"That is the point I've just made," said Uncle Maurice. "You'll find out everything in good time. Until then, what you don't know, you can't talk about. Now, when we get in, I want you to apologize to your mother for all the pain you've caused her. And promise her that nothing like that will ever happen again."

"But it will!" I burst out.

"No it won't," said Uncle Maurice firmly. "From now on, you're going to be a model citizen. No more attacks on Monsieur Armignac. No writing rude words about Germans on walls."

I shot Uncle Maurice a quick look at this, surprised. Was he just guessing, or did he really know that it was me who had painted anti-German slogans on one of the town walls?

"How will me being good get rid of the Germans?" I asked bitterly.

"That's what you're going to find out this afternoon," said Uncle Maurice secretively. "Oh, and another thing. Don't mention any of this to your mother."

"Mention any of what?" I asked, baffled. "I don't know anything."

"Good," said Uncle Maurice. "That's what I like to hear."

All the rest of the way home my head was in a whirl. What was Uncle Maurice talking about? For a moment I wondered if Uncle Maurice was talking about the Resistance, but that was impossible. The Resistance were fighters, men and women with machine guns who put their lives on the line and ambushed Germans in an effort to free our country. Uncle Maurice would have nothing to do with the Resistance. He had always kept on about leading a quiet life and not upsetting the enemy by opposing them. The way he had nodded in greeting to the German patrol just now showed he wasn't the man to stand up to them in any way. And nor were any of his friends. They were all the same sort: people who just wanted to lead a quiet life, who lived uncomplaining under German rule and did nothing to drive the enemy out.

So what was Uncle Maurice talking about bringing me in to? Maybe it was an organization like the Freemasons? Whatever it was and however he was involved, they would make sure I didn't misbehave in future. Perhaps they were planning to send me away to a juvenile prison.

With all these thoughts going round inside my head, I hardly noticed when we arrived home.

"Paul!"

My mother, as always, was in tears. But these were happy tears as she hugged me to her.

"Oh Paul, don't ever do that to me again," she said. "Promise me you'll stay out of trouble."

I looked over my mother's shoulder at Uncle Maurice, who gave me a firm glare.

"I promise, Mother," I said.

"Right," grumbled Uncle Maurice, "well, the bakery won't run itself. We'll have more of this hugging and kissing later. Right now I need Paul to help me in the bakery, and then I've promised Monsieur Limond to go and see him about an order for bread and cakes. I thought I'd take Paul with me – keep him out of trouble."

Mother look concerned at this. "Won't Monsieur Limond mind?" she asked. "After all, he is a very important person, and in view of his reputation, and with Paul just released from prison…"

Monsieur Limond was the wealthiest man in the area, a widower who lived in a huge house on the edge of Chinon. Not just a house, a mansion on an estate. To my mind Monsieur Limond was an enemy of France, because everyone knew that he let the German Commandant, General Fleischer, come inside his house and have tea with him. It was said that sometimes he and General Fleischer even sat down and ate a meal together. In my opinion this made Monsieur Limond a collaborator with the Germans, a traitor, and when the War was over I hoped he would be arrested and tried, or sent to prison for a long time.

"It will do Paul good to see how some people live – those who prefer to live a quiet life without making trouble," said Uncle Maurice.

As we went into the house, I wondered what lay in store for me at Monsieur Limond's house that afternoon. Perhaps Uncle Maurice was going to get rid of me by handing me over to Monsieur Limond to work on one of his farms. Well, I thought to myself sourly, if he thinks that, he can think again. There was no way I was going to work for a traitor. And even though I had promised my mother I wouldn't get into trouble again, I'd kept my fingers crossed as I'd said it, so it didn't count. Two weeks in prison hadn't dampened my spirits, nor my hatred of the Germans and my determination to push them out of my country; no matter what my uncle and Monsieur Limond might say or do to me.

I worked in the bakery all that morning, helping Uncle Maurice make the dough for the different sorts of bread, and the pastry for the croissants and cakes. With the shortages of flour and sugar because of the War, cakes particularly were in short supply and therefore in great demand. But Uncle Maurice said that bread must come first. People could live on bread, they couldn't live on cakes. So the flour that he could get hold of he used mainly for bread, and if he could get hold of any sugar then he made cakes, but usually only for "his special customers", as he called them.

As always, when I emptied the sacks of flour into the huge mixing bowl, it all came up in a cloud, filling my nose and turning my hair white. We worked for about four hours, with a break for coffee in the middle, and then my mother made us each a bowl of soup for lunch. We ate it with some of the fresh bread we'd made that morning.

After lunch, Uncle Maurice ordered me to brush the flour out of my hair and wash myself.

"Remember," he said, "we are seeing Monsieur Limond this afternoon. I don't want him to think my nephew is a ragamuffin as well as a violent criminal."

I opened my mouth to protest, then I saw the unhappy look on my mother's face, and I decided to keep quiet.

I cleaned myself up, and then we set off for Monsieur Limond's big house. I had thought we were going to walk the three miles, but to my surprise Uncle Maurice opened up his car, which he kept in a storehouse at the back of the bakery, and which he only ever used if he was delivering bread to an important customer. I noticed that, as well as bread, Uncle

Maurice had managed to make some cakes for Monsieur Limond, as well as bread rolls. I had no doubt that Monsieur Limond paid my uncle well for them.

My mother waved us goodbye as we set off and urged me, "not to let yourself down in front of Monsieur Limond". I nodded and assured her that I would be on my best behaviour.

When we arrived at Monsieur Limond's great house, the gates were open and we drove in and along an avenue of trees. Uncle Maurice parked his car round the back of the house and gestured for me to pick up the tray of pastries and carry it in.

Once inside I followed Uncle Maurice along a low-beamed corridor, and then into the kitchen. As I put the tray of pastries down on the table, I saw that there were three men already in the kitchen: Monsieur Limond himself – a large man wearing a velvet waistcoat and with a pair of spectacles hanging from a chain around his neck; his head gardener, an elderly and grim-faced man called Joseph who had once chased me off for scrumping apples from the trees in Monsieur Limond's orchard; and Monsieur Marchand, the father of Antoine, Jean and Denis. Of all of them, it was the presence of Monsieur Marchand that surprised me. What was he doing here? Then I remembered that he was a farmer. Perhaps he was here to do business with Monsieur Limond, but I was surprised nonetheless – surely Monsieur Marchand would not want to do business with someone like Monsieur Limond, who was friends with the Germans.

Monsieur Marchand smiled when he saw me.

"So," he grinned, "our fiery hero is back with us!"

"For which I hope he gives thanks to his uncle," growled Monsieur Limond.

"I do, sir," I said.

Monsieur Limond looked at me suspiciously, and then at Uncle Maurice.

"Are you sure he is reliable, Maurice?" he asked. "He is very headstrong."

"He will be safer inside than outside," said Maurice. "As you say, he is headstrong, and without a firm hand he will rush in on his own and cause all manner of mayhem."

"But I'll show the Germans that we can't be beaten down and used like slaves!" I said defiantly.

I waited for Monsieur Limond to get angry with me because I had attacked the Germans, but instead he turned to my uncle and said, "Let the boy wait outside while we talk about it."

Talk about what? I thought.

Uncle Maurice jerked with his thumb at the door, and I stepped out of the room. The door shut, and immediately I pressed my ear against it to find out what was being said about me. I heard Monsieur Limond ask: "Well, Joseph? What do you say?"

"There is no question that the boy is brave," came the

gardener's gruff voice. "The problem is that he is hot-headed. He does dangerous things. If he carries on as he is, he could ruin everything and take all of us down with him."

Down to where? I wanted to ask. What was all this talk about?

"But would you say he is intelligent?" asked Monsieur Limond.

"He certainly is!" put in Monsieur Marchand. "I have watched him helping my Antoine with his homework. There is no doubt in my mind that young Paul has all the brains that are needed."

"Very well," said Monsieur Limond. "Let's vote on it. Those for bringing him in?"

I couldn't see what was going on, but I guessed they were holding up hands to vote to "bring me in" to whatever it was they were talking about. I heard Monsieur Limond ask, "Those against?", and I heard Joseph snap grumpily, "I'll not vote against him. But I'll not vote for him, either. As I say, I think he's a hothead and dangerous."

"Trust me, Joseph, I can control him," said my uncle.

"Very well then," said Monsieur Limond. "We will bring him in."

I couldn't contain myself any more. Impatiently, I pushed open the door and demanded, "Into what?"

The four men looked at one another and shrugged. Monsieur Limond shook his head.

"I guessed that he would listen at the door, but obviously he is not that intelligent, or I think he might have worked it out by now. Though perhaps his stupidity could be our saving, if he was caught."

And then it hit me, and I looked round the room at the four of them, stunned.

"You're the Resistance!" I said, shocked.

"Just a small part," murmured Uncle Maurice. "There are more of us than you realize. So far we've been able to operate without too much interference from the Germans."

"They tolerate us because we don't cause trouble," interrupted Monsieur Limond with a half-smile.

"But the fuss you've been making lately could have changed all that, young Paul," added Joseph sternly.

My head was in a whirl. It didn't make sense. All the stories I'd heard about the Resistance happened in other parts of France, and were about groups of French patriots attacking German soldiers. None of this fitted with the four men in this room. Especially Monsieur Limond.

"What sort of resistance?" I demanded. "There have been no attacks on Germans in Chinon."

"Thank God for that, or our position would be impossible," chuckled Monsieur Marchand. "There'd be so many Germans here we'd never be able to get the British in and out."

I looked at him suspiciously. "In and out?" I repeated.

"He does that all the time," Uncle Maurice growled, annoyed. "Repeats things that people say. I find it very irritating."

"Before we go any further, I think we should ask the young man if he is going to join us or not," said Joseph.

"Yes!" I said fervently. "I'll do anything I can to rid our country of the Germans."

"Then, will you take an oath?" asked Monsieur Limond. "To swear to keep secret the names of any people you will meet and any actions you will witness?"

"I swear!" I said. "I won't reveal any secrets, not even if the Germans torture me!"

"Let's hope it won't come to that," said Monsieur Limond. "Here in Chinon we do not attack the Germans. As Monsieur Marchand has just explained. Because of that, the Germans leave this area alone. Or, at least, as alone as they can. They do not see us as causing trouble for them. This means we are able to use our area to return British pilots who have been shot down over France, and also to bring British spies in to France. From here they are able to get to other parts of France, gain as much information as possible, and then return home."

"The British and Americans are planning something big, Paul," put in Monsieur Marchand. "But for it to work, they need as much information as they can get on where the German strength is, where their weak points are, what sort of weapons they have, where their underground bunkers are."

I looked from one to the other, still in a bit of a daze as I took this in.

"But – but how long has this been going on?" I stammered. "I still can't believe that you are the Resistance."

"For two years," answered Monsieur Limond. "We admit what we have done for France hasn't been as spectacular as some of the Resistance cells around France – killing Germans and blowing up buildings – but our work has been vital. Air raids by the British and Americans have destroyed some important factories, stopping the Germans from developing their weapons. The information about those factories and what was being made there came from us."

"We pick up gossip: a bit here, a bit there," grunted Joseph. "Plus the chatter we get from the Germans as they come here to have tea with Monsieur Limond."

"Or when you deliver bread to them?" I said to Uncle Maurice.

Uncle Maurice nodded.

"Every word they say is reported back, no matter how unimportant it may appear," he said. "The British add everything up and build a big picture."

"How can I help?" I asked eagerly.

"We have had a message from London that there is someone coming in tonight," said Monsieur Limond. "You can help with that."

When I went to bed that night, I couldn't sleep for excitement about what lay before me. I was going to be working with the Resistance to bring a British spy into France. I – Paul Lelaud – was a member of the Resistance!

Before I went to bed, Uncle Maurice had said to my mother, "I'll be going out in the early hours to get more flour."

This wasn't unusual – bakers often worked through the night to make sure the bread was ready for first thing in the morning. And if Uncle Maurice heard that flour or salt had suddenly become available, he would go out in the night and return with the flour and salt, and then set to work making bread. It had never struck me that he had been doing anything other than his business as a baker, yet all the time he had been on missions with the Resistance! I could still hardly believe it of my uncle, who had always appeared so meek and so desperate not to upset the Germans.

"I'll take Paul with me," Uncle Maurice added.

My mother looked worried, and said, "Is that a good idea, Maurice?"

"Yes," grunted Maurice. "At least if he's with me I know he's not sneaking out and getting up to mischief."

So, at two in the morning, Uncle Maurice came into my room and told me it was time to wake up and get moving.

"I wasn't asleep," I told him as I got out of bed. "I'm too excited."

"Well don't say that sort of thing in front of your mother," grunted Uncle Maurice. "She'd wonder why collecting salt and flour at this time of night is so exciting."

We set off in his car towards the edge of town. As Uncle Maurice drove, I saw three German soldiers gathered on a street corner, their rifles held ready for action, and I tensed. But Uncle Maurice merely waved at them as we passed.

"They are so used to seeing me driving at this time of night to collect things for the bakery that they aren't suspicious," said Uncle Maurice. "And especially because I wave to them in a friendly manner. Why should they feel threatened by me?"

Suddenly lots of things made sense. The things that had made me angry about Uncle Maurice – the way he refused to stand up to the Germans or to Monsieur Armignac and the other French people who supported the Nazis – had all been a cover. Because he hadn't made threats against the Germans but had got on with making his bread for them and being polite to them, they thought he was "safe", so they left him alone. It was the same with

Monsieur Limond, because Monsieur Limond let the German Commandant, General Fleischer, into his house for meals and to take tea.

We left the town, and then Uncle Maurice drove along a lot of narrow country roads. We drove slowly because Uncle Maurice had turned his lights off so as not to draw attention to us. After what seemed like ages, we turned off on to a track, which we followed, bumping over the uneven ground until we came to a gate.

"Open the gate," said Uncle Maurice. "Then close it again after I've taken the car in."

As I was doing as he'd asked, I saw the dim shape of another car already in the field. Then I realized that Joseph and his son, André, were coming towards us. Both of them had rifles.

"Everything is ready," said Joseph as my uncle joined us. "They should be here in the next ten minutes."

Uncle Maurice nodded. "We won't take chances," he said. "We'll wait for five minutes before we light the fires, unless we hear the plane, in which case we'll light them sooner. Paul and I will light the fires, if you and André keep watch."

Joseph nodded, and he and André separated and began to work their way round the edge of the field in opposite directions.

I looked after André enviously. "Can I have a gun?" I asked.

"No," replied Uncle Maurice sharply.

"But André has a gun and he's only a year older than me," I protested.

"André has been using a rifle since he was six years old," my uncle replied. "You've never handled a gun before. If you start now, the bundle of nerves you are, you're more likely to shoot one of us. Or the British agent. Your job is to help me light the fires that will show the plane the way. Follow me."

Uncle Maurice headed towards the middle of the field. As I walked behind him, I tripped in a deep furrow and fell down.

"Lucky you weren't carrying a gun if you're going to be clumsy like that," said Uncle Maurice. "You'd have shot yourself."

"The ground is all uneven," I complained as I got to my feet. "It's been ploughed up." Then a thought struck me. "It's going to be difficult for a plane to land here with all these furrows."

"That's exactly why we use it," said Uncle Maurice. "The Germans won't expect a ploughed field like this to be used for planes landing or taking off."

He could see that I was still puzzled, so he added: "The plane isn't going to land. It flies in and then, when it's just above the ground, the agent jumps out."

"Jumps?" I echoed, shocked. "Don't they hurt themselves?"

"Sometimes," said Uncle Maurice. "But most times they just land and roll over on the ground to take the shock. They're trained how to fall."

"But I thought they came down by parachute," I said.

"Parachutes can be unreliable," said Uncle Maurice. "They can get blown off course. This way, the agents land where they want to land."

We walked in silence across the dark field, me stumbling every now and then as my foot plunged down into one of the deep furrows made by the plough.

The whole time we walked my heart was thumping with fear. The Germans might catch us at any time. What would we say if they came now and saw us? We'd be shot for sure.

We had almost reached the middle of the field, when I saw something sticking up out of the ground. As we got nearer I saw that it was a stick.

"Careful," said Uncle Maurice. "Where the stick is marks a hole in the ground. Don't fall into it."

We reached the hole, and Uncle Maurice pulled the stick out. By now my eyes had become accustomed to the darkness, and I could just about make out some broken shapes at the bottom of the hole, and a smell of paraffin.

"This is the first hole," explained Uncle Maurice. "There are four of them, all filled with wood soaked in paraffin. The wood's in holes so that when the fires start up they won't be seen except from the air.

"When all four are lit they show as four corners of a box. The plane is going to drop the agent in that box.

When I give the word, you light the wood in this hole." He handed me a box of matches. "Remember, there's paraffin on the wood to help the fires start, so make sure you don't burn yourself. As soon as you've done that, walk about forty paces along this furrow until you come to another hole, then light the wood in that hole. I'll set light to the two holes on the other side."

"What do we do after we've lit the fires?" I asked.

"You keep well back, unless you want to get knocked down and killed by a low-flying plane," Uncle Maurice replied. "Stay over by the hedge at the side of the field. Once the agent's on the ground and the plane has gone, we go back and fill in the holes with earth to put out the fires. While we're doing that, Joseph and André will be taking care of the agent."

"Shall I light my fire now?" I asked, opening the box of matches.

"Not yet," said Uncle Maurice. "The less time we have the fires alight, the less chance there is of anyone noticing us."

He stood there, and even in the darkness I could see that he was listening out for the sound of the aircraft, his head slightly to one side. I couldn't hear anything other than the usual sounds at night: the rustling of wind in the leaves and small animals hurrying through undergrowth.

"There it is!" said Uncle Maurice. "Quick! Start the fires!"

I struck my match and dropped it in, and immediately the paraffin caught light. Uncle Maurice was already running across the ploughed field to his first hole.

I hurried along the furrow, counting paces as I did, stumbling all the time … 20 paces, 21, 22… 35, 36, 37… And then I nearly fell into the second hole. I stopped myself just in time, struck a match, and dropped it into the hole. My heart nearly stopped as I saw the match just simply go out. No fire! Maybe they had forgotten to put paraffin on the wood in this hole? How would I get it started? My fingers were trembling as I struck my second match, and this time I lowered it into the hole, rather than dropping it on the wood. As it touched the timber, the paraffin suddenly lit with a bang, and I fell back in alarm.

"Quick, Paul!" called my uncle, as he ran up to me. "Get out of the way!"

He grabbed me by the shoulder and hustled me across the ploughed field. I could now hear something behind us, up in the sky. It was an engine, but I could tell from the sound of it that all was not well.

"There's something wrong with the plane!" I said, alarmed. "Listen to it, the engine's making a popping noise!"

"The pilot's doing that on purpose," said Uncle Maurice. "He's making it sound like a motorcycle engine, so if anyone hears it no one will think it's a plane."

We stopped, and I looked around. I couldn't see the four

fires, but I could smell them, the scent of burning paraffin and wood coming thickly in waves of smoke across the field. My heart started thumping again. Surely if we could smell the fires, others could as well. A German patrol would smell them for sure!

Then I was aware of a large shape looming up in the night sky, its wings wide. It was the biggest thing I had ever seen. There were no lights showing on it. Down down down it came, lower and lower, and I could hear the sound of its engine slowing and I thought with alarm, "If it goes any slower it will crash in the field, and what will we do then?"

And then I saw something fall out from the plane and roll over the ground. The plane began to rise up, and then the sounds of its engine revved up faster for just a second. Then there came that peculiar popping noise again, just like a motorcycle engine, and then the plane soared away into the darkness.

"Quick! Put out your fires!" said my uncle.

We hurried towards the centre of the field. Joseph was also running. André was nowhere to be seen, so I guessed he was still keeping watch, his rifle at the ready.

As I got near to my fires, I saw the figure that had fallen out of the plane stand up. As I got nearer, I could see that it was a woman. She raised a hand in greeting to Joseph and Maurice, and then hurried off with Joseph towards where his car was waiting.

I set to work kicking earth into the holes, putting out the fires. All the time I felt a great sense of excitement. I had helped my first British agent land. I had struck my first proper blow against the Germans!

By the time Uncle Maurice and I had put our fires out and returned to his car, Joseph was just driving out of the field. André had opened the gate for him and Joseph slowed down to let him get in and then drove off.

"Remember to shut the gate after us," Uncle Maurice called to me. "It's remembering the little details that keep us safe."

As we drove away from the field, I asked excitedly: "What happens now?"

"We go and get some sacks of flour," said Uncle Maurice.

"Oh," I said, disappointed.

"That's what we said we were going to do," Uncle Maurice reminded me. "It would look very suspicious if we came back without any, especially if we run into the same German patrol that saw us leave town."

"True," I admitted. But my curiosity, which was bursting in me, couldn't be contained. "But that woman," I demanded. "The agent. Is she really from England? Or is she French? What will happen to her? Where is she going? What's her mission?"

"Paul, a very important thing to remember is that you never ask questions," said Uncle Maurice sternly. "The less you know, the less you can tell if they catch you."

I gave a sigh, but fell silent. Although I knew that what

my uncle said made sense, I wanted to know these things. I wanted to know that what we were doing was making a difference, that it was going to bring the end to having the Germans in our country. I wanted to know that my father hadn't died in vain. After three years of occupation, I wanted to know that we were going to be free.

After all the excitement of that night, I slept late. I felt terribly guilty when I woke up and saw the sun streaming in through the window, and I could hear the sound of Uncle Maurice working in the bakery below. I hurried downstairs, and bumped into my mother in the kitchen.

"I'm sorry I slept so late, Mother," I said. "You should have woken me."

"Your uncle and I felt you needed the sleep, Paul," she said. "After working with him last night ... and suffering the way you did in that dreadful police cell these past weeks."

I didn't have the heart to tell her that I hadn't suffered at all, that I'd had a very easy time of it. Sergeant Boulet had made sure I was fed, and when he realized how bored I was, he made sure I had a newspaper to read, or a pack of cards to play with. In fact, despite the fear that I'd felt, I spent so much time just lounging on the bed in my cell, it was possibly the laziest two weeks I'd spent in years.

"I must go and help Uncle Maurice," I said. "He didn't get much sleep either last night, collecting the flour."

As I went to go through into the shop, my mother stopped me.

"I'm glad that you and your uncle seem to be getting on better," she said. "You always seemed so resentful towards him. But he does his best."

He certainly does, I thought. My uncle is a secret hero of the Resistance.

For the rest of the morning I helped Uncle Maurice prepare the dough for the bread. While we were doing it, Antoine, Denis and Jean Marchand arrived.

"Hello, Monsieur Dubonne," Antoine greeted Uncle Maurice. "We came to see how Paul was."

"Busy," grunted Uncle Maurice, and if I hadn't seen a different side of Uncle Maurice I'd have thought he was just the same sour man I'd always known. Then he gave a shrug. "But he can have a short break, providing he doesn't get up to mischief."

"I won't, Uncle," I promised.

I took off my flour-covered apron, and hung it on a hook, and then my friends and I went outside to the street.

"Well?" demanded Denis eagerly.

"Well what?" I asked, puzzled.

"What was it like being in prison?" asked Denis.

"Did they torture you?" asked Jean.

"Don't be silly," I said. "I was in the charge of Sergeant Boulet, not the Gestapo." Then, suddenly curious, I asked: "What's happened at school?"

"Oh, school's finished," said Antoine. "Monsieur Armignac had to go to hospital for treatment. You broke his nose and blackened both his eyes, and someone said you may have even broken one of his ribs."

"Good," I said fervently.

"What did your uncle and mother say about it?" asked Denis.

"Oh, they were pretty good about it," I said. "Mother got very upset, but Uncle Maurice just told me not to do it again."

"That's because he doesn't want to upset the Germans," sneered Antoine. "He's just like our father. None of them want to do anything to upset the Nazis."

I wanted to shout out at him: "That's where you're so wrong! Your father and my uncle are heroes of the Resistance!" but I had to stop myself. And then I realized what Uncle Maurice meant about not knowing too much. The temptation to tell Antoine what had happened the previous night, helping the British agent land, was so strong. I wanted to boast about what I'd done, to let him know that ordinary French people were fighting to free our country, but I couldn't. If I told him, he might tell Denis and Jean, and they might tell someone else, as proud of their father as I was of my uncle, and soon someone might hear about it who was a supporter of the Germans, and that would be the end. My uncle and Antoine's father and

Monsieur Limond, along with Joseph and me and André, would be taken away and shot. And all because I couldn't keep a secret.

But I will keep this secret, I vowed to myself. No one will ever find out anything from me.

For the next few weeks I waited for news about the spy who had landed in the field. I wondered if she had got to where she was going. Had she been captured by the Gestapo? Would she be coming back so we could get her out of the country? If so, how would that work? Would the British plane land this time, or would she try and get back on board while it was flying low? So many questions, and no answers. Uncle Maurice had made it clear to me that I wasn't to bother him, and so I just kept my excitement to myself and got on with day-to-day work in the bakery. All the time I was waiting for Uncle Maurice to tell me that there was a "special collection" to be made at night, but he never said anything. It was all very frustrating.

I was excited when Uncle Maurice took me to Monsieur Limond's house about a week after we had helped the British agent land, thinking that we were about to do something similar again, but this visit was to show me how to work the secret radio set.

"There may come a day when we have to get important messages out, or receive them, and we may all be busy," Uncle Maurice told me.

The radio was kept buried beneath a haystack inside one of the barns. Even if the Germans had poked rifles into the haystack they wouldn't have found it, because it was hidden in a hole in the ground beneath the hay.

Joseph and André took the radio out of its hiding place and set it on a bench. It was a funny-looking piece of equipment: a square metal box with thin metal cables going from it to a large metal hoop that was hanging from the barn door.

"That hoop is the aerial," explained André. "On its own, without the wires leading to it, it just looks like the rim of a wheel, or something."

I must admit, I felt a bit jealous of André as I watched him put the headphones on, and then start tapping his fingers on a metal knob, which banged on to a metal plate every time he touched it. Here he was, not much older than me, and he was using a radio to send secret messages!

"This is a key for sending a message by Morse code," André said. "It takes a while to learn the code, but it's necessary."

"Do you think you can learn the code, Paul?" asked Joseph.

"Of course," I said, stiffly. I felt that if André could pick this up, so could I.

"Every time you bang the knob it sends a signal. If you bang it lightly, then that's just a short signal, which is a dot when it's written down at the other end. If you hold the key down for longer, then that's a longer signal, and it reads as a dash. Together, the dots and dashes mean different letters. For example, the letter "S" is made up of three dots, and the letter "O" is made up of three dashes. So if you wanted to send "SOS" – which means we need help urgently – then you'd send three dots, then three dashes, then three dots."

"It's not as easy as André makes it seem," said Uncle Maurice. "He does it well because he's been doing it for quite a while."

"I'm not as good at it as André," admitted Joseph. "It needs someone younger, with nimble fingers on the key. And good hearing to be able to hear the dots and dashes when there's a message coming in from the other end."

"Want to try?" offered André.

I took his place on the stool in front of the radio, and put the headphones on. For the next few minutes I listened as whoever was at the other end sent a test message, and tried to distinguish between short clicks (dots) and long buzzes (dashes), and tried to keep up with writing down what I heard. The sounds all seemed to come over the headphones very quickly. Even as I wrote down dot and dashes, I knew I was making mistakes, and I felt angry with myself for getting it wrong.

I'd only been doing it for a few minutes when Joseph began to unplug the wires from the radio and to wrap them up.

"I was just getting the hang of it," I protested. "Let me stay on!"

"We can't stay on too long in case the Germans pick up the signal," explained Joseph. "They have equipment that can trace where radio messages are being sent from."

I helped Uncle Maurice move the hay to one side while Joseph and André disconnected the radio and put it back in its hiding place.

"Don't worry about not getting it right first time," said Uncle Maurice. "It took André quite a while, didn't it, André?"

André nodded.

"I used to practise with a nail," he said. "You hold the nail, and tap it – a short tap for a dot, holding it down for a dash. It's helps a lot and if anyone spots you they don't know what you're doing. They think you're just tapping out a tune, or something."

"OK," I nodded. "I'll practise tapping with a nail. When can I have another go on the radio?"

"Soon," said Joseph. "We have to be careful about using it too often. Next time you come, you can sit with André and watch him while he sends and takes messages."

"I don't want to watch André", I thought angrily. "I want to do it myself." But I didn't say anything. Joseph had already said he thought I was too headstrong, too impatient. It was up to me to prove him wrong.

As soon as we got home I took the code that André had written out for me, a list of which dots and dashes meant which letter, and began to practise in my room. Unfortunately, my mother got fed up with what she called my "constant tapping" which was giving her a headache, so from then on I worked on the Morse code away from the house.

I did have one more session with André at the radio, but I never got the chance to do it myself. I just had to be content with sitting and watching him tapping, and writing down dots and dashes. I did my best to work out the message as quickly as I could, but André was still quicker than me.

One day in August, news came that turned the whole of our world in Chinon upside down.

My mother was serving in the shop and Uncle Maurice and I were bringing in trays of bread, when the shop door opened and Madame Vallon came in. Madame Vallon was in her fifties, a nervous sort of woman at the best of times. Now she was in a very distressed state.

"Have you heard the news?" she asked, her voice fearful.

"No," said my mother, intrigued.

"Sergeant Boulet has been shot."

Sergeant Boulet! I felt sick on hearing this. Sergeant Boulet, who had been so kind to me when I had been in his prison.

"The Germans?" I asked.

Madame Vallon shook her head.

"No," she replied, "they say the Resistance did it."

The Resistance?

I looked across at Uncle Maurice, stunned at this news, but he simply shook his head once, firmly, then said: "Paul, come and give me a hand with the salt."

As I followed him out of the shop, I heard Madame Vallon saying to my mother in a terrified voice: "He was in a car with a patrol of three German soldiers. They were ambushed by gunmen just outside Chinon." She groaned, loudly and miserably. "This will mean terrible revenge from the Germans."

As soon as Uncle Maurice and I were out of earshot of my mother and Madame Vallon, I demanded angrily, "Why?"

"The Resistance did not do this," said Uncle Maurice curtly. "If what she says is true, then it is the work of the Maquis."

"But the Maquis and the Resistance are on the same side," I said.

Uncle Maurice shook his head.

"We're supposed to be on the same side, fighting the Germans, but we have different methods," he said. "It's true that some Resistance groups have attacked Germans, but most work as we do here in Chinon. We help captured British airmen escape back to England. We help spies in and out of France. Now and then we carry out sabotage to slow down the German war machine: break railway lines, cut telephone cables. But mostly we work without the Germans being aware of what we are doing, right under their very noses.

"The Maquis think there is only one way to drive the Germans out, and that is to kill them. Shoot them. Blow them up. Assassinations."

"But why would they kill Sergeant Boulet? He was no German sympathizer. He was good to me when I was in jail."

"To the Maquis, anyone who works with the Germans is a target. Sergeant Boulet was with a German patrol, so as far as they're concerned he was an enemy. Anyway, we don't know the facts yet. Only what Madame Vallon has told us."

We found out later that Madame Vallon had been perfectly right. Sergeant Boulet had been visiting a farm about five miles from Chinon, checking on a rumour that a local farmer had a gun without a proper licence. Although all farmers used to have guns to shoot rabbits and foxes and pigeons, since the Germans had occupied France, all guns were forbidden, unless the owner had a licence from them. Very few people had such licences. I learnt from Uncle Maurice that Monsieur Limond was allowed to keep the guns on his estates, because he let the German Commandant hunt on his land, and because the Germans trusted him. That was how Joseph and André had been able to bring guns with them on that particular night when we helped the agent land: if they had been stopped, they could have said they were shooting foxes to protect Monsieur Limond's hens, and they would have had German-issued licences to back them up.

Anyway, Sergeant Boulet had found nothing at the farm and he had been returning to Chinon with the German soldiers, when they ran into an ambush. A car had been placed across the road, forcing them to slow down. As they did so, some men jumped out from the hedges on both sides of the road and sprayed the car with bullets from sub-machine guns. One of the soldiers survived long enough to report all this before he died.

The shooting left me with mixed feelings. On one hand I was pleased that the Germans had been shot, but I felt very sad about Sergeant Boulet. He had only been doing his job, and he had done nothing to help the Germans since they'd arrived.

Uncle Maurice didn't have any mixed feelings at all.

"The Maquis have ruined it for us!" he said angrily. "You see, the Germans will step down on us. It will be even harder to carry out our work. And they will seek revenge. It's happened in other towns where German soldiers have been shot. And now it comes to Chinon."

A week later the ambush notices went up all over town. They read: "By order of Commandant Geutler, all people of Chinon are ordered to assemble in the town square at 12 noon on Saturday 21 August. Failure to join the assembly will be seen as an act of war against the German Reich and any offenders will be arrested and executed."

"What is going to happen?" asked my mother, nervously.

"I hear they have rounded up twenty men," said Uncle Maurice, anger making his voice tremble. "They are going to be shot. The Germans have fixed a rate of five dead for each of the men the Maquis killed in the ambush."

"They can't!" moaned my mother. "They surely don't think these twenty men carried out the shootings."

"The Germans don't care if they did or not," said Uncle Maurice. And, with a deep sigh, he added: "It could be worse. After one German was killed in Bordeaux, the Germans shot a hundred people in Bordeaux, Chateaubriant and Nantes."

"Is – is there anyone we know among the twenty?" asked my mother.

Uncle Maurice nodded.

"Guillaume Vallon, Albert Fouchard, Robert Lestair and Jules Douvin. The other sixteen I don't really know personally, although I know most of them or their families by name."

"Guillaume Vallon?" repeated my mother, shocked. "Oh no! Poor Denise! Isn't there some way this can be stopped, Maurice? Can't you talk to the Mayor, or Monsieur Limond? They have influence with the Germans. They can get Commandant Fleischer to stop this from happening."

Uncle Maurice shook his head.

"It's no longer Fleischer who's in charge," he said. "After the ambush, the SS took over. Commandant Geutler now rules. Fleischer has been replaced."

"But this can't be allowed to happen!" burst out my mother. "There must be a way to stop it!"

"There is no way, Angeline," said my uncle firmly. "It's going to happen. If we try and stop it, more of us will be killed."

"At least we can stay away from it," said my mother. "I don't want to see that horrible thing happening."

"We can't," said Uncle Maurice. "Remember what the notice said: 'Failure to join the assembly will be seen as an act of war against the German Reich and any offenders will be arrested and executed.' We have to go."

"But not Paul," insisted my mother. "He's just a child!"

"That's the whole point," said Uncle Maurice sadly. "The SS want the children to see their fathers and uncles and brothers executed. They're sending out a message about what will happen to all of them if they try and fight back."

On Saturday, 21 August, we all gathered in the town square. The Germans had miscalculated – there were thousands of people, far too many for the town square, so they put up road blocks to stop more people from coming in. Unfortunately we had got there early because my uncle thought they might start rounding up people who were staying away, and he didn't want us to get arrested. So, at twelve o'clock, noon, we were already in the square, along with thousands of others.

Four tanks were in the square, their huge guns aimed at the crowd. Ranks of German soldiers lined up the whole way around it, their rifles pointed menacingly at us. The Germans were making absolutely sure that we knew that if any kind of riot broke out, we'd all be massacred.

On one side of the square a large space had been cleared, and a row of German soldiers, rifles on their shoulders, marched into it. I could hear the rigid tramping of their boots, and just see them between the shoulders of the people in front of me.

"Don't look, Paul!" my mother whispered urgently beside me.

I closed my eyes, but then I opened them again, just enough. I couldn't stop myself from watching what was going on.

A command was shouted out, and the line of marching soldiers stopped and stood to attention. Another shouted a command, and the soldiers swung round as one to face the wall at the side of the square.

Into the arena strode the figure of Commandant Geutler. It was the first time I'd set eyes on him. He was dressed in a tight black uniform, with lots of silver and gold on his jacket. Under his black cap, his face was deathly white. "SS," muttered a voice near me in the crowd.

Then I noticed the difference. The former German Commandant in Chinon, Commandant Fleischer, had worn a grey uniform: grey cap, grey jacket and trousers, grey overcoat. That was the uniform of the German Army. The SS were said to be Hitler's own private army. They wore black to show they were special. They had more power than the officers in the regular German Army.

Geutler walked up the steps of the Town Hall so that he was above us. A microphone had been set up for him, and he went over to it.

"People of Chinon," he announced, his voice ringing out from the speakers set up around the square. "An act of murder has been committed against the German Army here in this town. We will catch the criminals who carried out this act and punish them. But, as a warning to any others of you who may be stupid enough to try and repeat this act, this is what will happen to you, and to those you claim to care for. Today, we will shoot five citizens of Chinon for every German killed. They killed four, we will shoot twenty. If it happens again, then the next time we will execute ten men for every German or French official killed. Let this be a warning to you all. Heil Hitler."

With that, Geutler made the Nazi salute with his arm, and then followed it with a brief gesture towards where a group of soldiers were waiting at one side of the square.

A drum began beating slowly and I heard the sound of shuffling feet, and then – between the bodies of the crowd in front of me – I saw a line of men being pushed along by a row of armed soldiers. I recognized Monsieur Vallon, third in the line, and then from behind me I heard a terrible wailing sound.

"Guillaume! Guillaume! No!"

I realized it was Madame Vallon crying out.

A German officer – like Geutler, also dressed in black – strode to the microphone and barked into it: "There will be no outbursts! Anyone shouting out will be arrested!"

But this didn't shut up Madame Vallon. She kept on crying and yelling out her husband's name. "Guillaume! Guillaume!"

The German officer on the steps snapped an order at the soldiers near him, and in a second they were charging towards us. They barged through the crowd, knocking people aside with the butts of their rifles.

I turned and saw them reach the wailing figure of Madame Vallon. They grabbed her roughly and dragged her through the crowd, out towards the front. As the crowd parted in front of me, I saw Monsieur Vallon stop in the line of shuffling men and turn towards her, and then start to move, but the German soldier nearest to him clubbed him with his rifle, and Monsieur Vallon fell to the ground, clutching his head.

The soldiers who had hold of Madame Vallon half-dragged her out of the crowd, and headed towards a door that led into the side of the Town Hall.

Commandant Geutler returned to the microphone. An unhappy murmuring began to rumble among the crowd.

"If there are any further disturbances, I will order my men to bring out another ten men from the crowd and they will also be shot!" he snapped.

The rumbling from the crowd died down to an awkward silence.

The soldiers hauled Monsieur Vallon to his feet, and then they shepherded him and the other nineteen men over to the wall. Even at this stage I couldn't believe they were really going to shoot them. These were innocent men. They had done nothing wrong. They hadn't written slogans on walls against the Germans, or probably even said anything bad about them, they had just got on with their lives under the occupation as much as they could. And now they were being lined up against a wall to be shot.

The soldiers stepped away from them. Next, the line of soldiers that had been standing to attention facing the wall turned to the line of twenty civilian men: some old, some young, some middle-aged. All of them looked terrified, except for one elderly man in the middle of the line, who stood stiffly to attention.

"Who's that man in the middle?" I whispered to Uncle

Maurice. "The old one with the brown jacket, standing up so straight."

"Paul, I told you to close your eyes!" came my mother's horrified whisper to me.

"That's Andre Baptiste," replied Uncle Maurice in very low tones. "He was a hero of the Great War. He won many medals. After that he became a teacher. He's a very wise and brave man."

I looked at the men, at Monsieur Baptiste, standing straight and tall, at Monsieur Vallon, leaning against the wall to help him stay upright, blood trickling down his face from the wound where the soldier had hit him, and at the others: some of whom stood stiff, while others cringed and cowered. I wondered how I would behave if it had been me. I couldn't understand why they just stood there, why they didn't run.

"Ready!" shouted the commander of the line of soldiers, and each man smartly put his rifle to his shoulder.

"Take aim!" shouted the commander.

And then I heard the strangest and most moving noise: it was the sound of singing, and I realized that it was Monsieur Baptiste's voice I could hear, and he was singing our national anthem, "La Marseillaise". Then, another man in the line joined him, and then another, and I felt a lump in my throat and tears sprang into my eyes as I saw these men, facing death, singing about how our country would never be ruled by tyrants, and I found myself singing along too. And then, the rest of the crowd began to sing, and as one we sang, tears pouring down our faces…

"Fire!"

The sound of the soldiers' rifles exploded in the square, and the singing stopped, and there was just silence, broken only by the sound of sobbing from the crowd.

SEPTEMBER – OCTOBER 1943

The whole of our town was in shock after the executions in the town square. For days afterwards no one could talk of anything else, but when they did it was in whispered tones, afraid of being overheard by the Germans.

The sight of our oppressors shooting all those brave men brought back memories of the night in the railway station, when they'd killed that woman. I recalled Emile and his family standing on the platform, the German soldier hitting Monsieur Levy and then pushing Emile and the others into the cattle trucks – just because they were Jewish. It didn't make sense. It was like rounding up people because they were left-handed, or they had red hair. Emile now seemed so very far away, and not just in miles. It was as if he'd been snatched out of my life and I would never see him again. This thought brought tears to my eyes, and I pushed the idea away. Of course I would see him again. Once this war was over we'd get together and talk about how awful our experiences had been, but all that would be behind us. In the future, we'd be able to laugh again and have fun, and it would be as good as it always had been between us. But right now, that future seemed to be a long, long way away.

After Commandant Geutler took over from General Fleischer, there were more German patrols, more people being stopped on the street and taken in for questioning. Those who were rounded up were taken to the SS Headquarters, which had been set up in the Town Hall. Some were released, but others were kept and interrogated. There were rumours that they were tortured to make them give names of people who were in the Resistance. Some of them named names, not because they knew anything, but because they wanted the torture to stop. Those who were named were then arrested and taken to the Town Hall and interrogated. Most of them were released, without charge, but all of them looked scared afterwards.

Of all the names that came out, none of them were of Uncle Maurice, or Monsieur Marchand, or Monsieur Limond, or Joseph or André. All of them appeared to be law-abiding citizens, keen to work with the Germans, and above suspicion. They had been careful not to let anyone into their group who might be impetuous or hot-headed, or someone who might get into trouble. Except me.

Commandant Geutler did not go to Monsieur Limond's house for meals or tea as General Fleischer had done. The SS Commandant stayed in the Town Hall most of the time, and if he wanted to see people they were brought to him.

"It will be much harder to get people in or out now, Paul," Uncle Maurice whispered to me one day in October. "The Germans are keeping a closer eye on everything, following up every report or rumour of anything suspicious. We've been lucky we haven't had to move anyone these past few weeks."

Because there was no major activity for the Resistance after the executions in the Town Square, things quietened down for me. A couple of times I went to Monsieur Limond's to work with André on the radio. Once he actually let me send a message. It was just a short one, but I got it right and I felt really proud. Especially when the person at the other end in England signed off with "Courage, comrades". They must have thought I was an adult, one of their comrades, and not just a 14-year-old boy. I felt so proud to be part of this movement and was sure we were going to push the Germans out of France for ever.

A couple of times I cycled over to the Marchand's farm to see Antoine, but both times Antoine was busy working with his father on the farm and I couldn't interrupt him.

Then the British agent came back. The first clue I had was when Joseph came into Uncle Maurice's shop. He looked his usual sour self and, after buying two loaves of bread from my mother, he said to Uncle Maurice: "Oh, and Monsieur Limond wants you to deliver some cakes to his house this afternoon. He's got a cousin from Paris come to stay for a few days, and he wants to give her tea."

"A cousin?" asked my mother. "Really? How old is she? What sort of cakes does she like? How long is she staying? What does she do in Paris?"

"Really, Angeline," protested Uncle Maurice. "You're as bad as the police with all these questions."

"That's all right, Maurice," grunted Joseph. "She works as a temporary teacher, filling in at different schools when the regular teachers are sick. She's just finished at one school, so she thought she'd come down here into the country for a few days."

"Well, tell Monsieur Limond we'll make up a selection of cakes for her," my mother assured Joseph.

"Thank you, madame," said Joseph, and with that he left.

Afterwards, when Uncle Maurice and I were in the workshop behind the bakery, he winked at me.

"Clever, huh?" he smiled. "Did you notice who else was in the shop when Joseph talked about Monsieur Limond's cousin?"

I nodded.

"Madame Gabin and Monsieur Entrait," I replied.

"Exactly," said Uncle Maurice. "The two biggest gossips in Chinon. If the Germans get curious about the mystery woman who's staying with Monsieur Limond, within a few hours they'll have found out that she's just a cousin of his, a teacher taking a break from Paris. With luck they won't dig any deeper."

"But what if they do?" I asked.

"Don't worry," said Uncle Maurice. "This woman is an expert at what she does. If they check on her, they'll find she has taught at schools in Paris."

That afternoon, Uncle Maurice took me with him when he set off for Monsieur Limond's house with a selection of small cakes he had made with his reserve store of sugar. My mother had helped him decide which cakes to make. Because I was going to be meeting this "cousin" from Paris, my mother even made me wash my hands and face and change into my smartest clothes before we set off.

When we arrived at the big house, I carried the tray of cakes into the kitchen. The British agent was sitting in the kitchen with Monsieur Limond, and she smiled at me as I came in.

"Hello, again," she said.

This was the first time I'd had a chance to see her properly. I guessed she was about 30, with long black hair swept back from her forehead in waves. Her clothes were smart, but not too expensive-looking. Just right for a teacher. For a spy she seemed very much at ease – cool and calm. Though I suppose that's how spies looked.

"We never got a chance to say hello properly before, or for me to say thank you," she said, and she stood up and held out her hand to me.

I could feel my face burning red with embarrassment as I

took her hand and shook it, bowing my head as I did so. For an Englishwoman, her French was perfect.

"I see you have brought a good selection of cakes," smiled Monsieur Limond. "A rarity these days."

"My sister insisted," said Uncle Maurice. "She heard about your cousin arriving, and wanted to make sure she gets a good impression of Chinon hospitality."

"Good," nodded Monsieur Limond.

Then he gestured towards two of the empty chairs at the kitchen table.

"Sit," he said. "We can eat as we talk."

We joined them at the kitchen table. A large teapot was in the middle of the table, under a knitted tea cosy to keep the tea warm. Monsieur Limond poured for us, and as he did he introduced me to the agent.

"Allow me to introduce my cousin, Françoise Literre," he announced. To the woman, he said, "Our baker friend, you have already met. The young man is his nephew."

"My name is – " I began, but she cut me off quickly.

"Your name is Pierre, of course," she said cheerfully.

I was baffled. Pierre? And then I understood. What an idiot I was! Of course, I doubt if any of the names being used were real, just in case word leaked out. Monsieur Limond, of course, would use his real name because she was staying in his house. And the same would go for Joseph and André. But for the rest, the people of Chinon outside Monsier Limond's household, she would be calling them by aliases.

"Françoise has a job for us," announced Monsieur Limond, and my heart leapt. I was going into action again!

The cakes on the table were forgotten as I sat and watched this secret agent tell us about her mission.

"A high-ranking German officer will be coming here soon," she said. "Our job is to get him out of France and on a plane to England."

A German officer? I was puzzled. "Why?" I blurted out.

"Don't ask questions!" snapped my uncle disapprovingly.

"No, that's all right," smiled the woman known as Françoise. "It might help him if he knows how important this mission is."

Turning to me, she said: "There are many high-ranking German officers who believe that Germany will lose the War. Rather than see their army and their country destroyed, some of them are keen to negotiate a peace. This officer is one of them. He's acting as a go-between for even more senior officers in the German Army in their negotiations with the British and American Governments. As proof of their good intent, he is bringing with him certain documents. It's vital that this officer, and the documents he's carrying, get to England."

I nodded.

"Thank you for trusting in me," I said. "I apologize for asking questions."

"No apology needed," she smiled.

"In that case, I have a question," said Monsieur Limond. "I assume this German officer will have to be hidden here on my estate?"

Françoise nodded.

"For how long?" asked Monsieur Limond. "Ever since Commandant Geutler and the SS have taken command of this area, things have become much more dangerous. They could come poking around here at any time."

"I don't know," Françoise replied. "He's being sent here with the help of different Resistance groups, so I can't tell you when he's going to arrive. It could be a few days. It could be a week. When he does get here, he'll give the codeword 'Sparrow'. If he says that word to any of you and I'm not here, let me know at once. I've met this officer already, so I'll be able to confirm that he really is the correct man. Once I've done that, I'll radio England and arrange transport. Because they want to get him there very badly, they won't let him stay here long. Three days at the most, I expect."

"In that case we'd better get things organized," said Monsieur Limond. "The people here already know about this situation, but our other friend, Monsieur Pommeline," (I assumed he was referring to Monsieur Marchand) "needs to be told. It might not be advisable for me or my people to call at this moment. You never know when it might arouse suspicion. Would you and young ... Pierre ... go and see him?"

"Of course," nodded Uncle Maurice. "We'll call on him on our way back to town."

Uncle Maurice and I stood up, and he bowed politely to the woman who called herself Françoise.

"Goodbye, Mademoiselle," he said. "We will meet again soon."

"Thank you," she smiled. "And thank you for the cakes."

After we left Monsieur Limond's house we drove straight to the Marchands' farm. I was pleased because it would give me a chance to see Antoine, Denis and Jean again. What with working at the bakery, and everyone too afraid to go far from home after the killings in the town square, I hadn't seen much of them. And Antoine had been too busy recently working with his father to have time to spare for me.

As we approached, I saw Madame Marchand in the yard hanging washing out on the line. Antoine, Denis and Jean were in the barn, stacking bales of hay. We pulled up in the car and got out.

"Maurice!" exclaimed Madame Marchand. "How are you?"

"Very well," smiled Uncle Maurice. "Is Jacques in?"

"He's in the kitchen, doing some paperwork," said Madame Marchand. "Come inside. You too, Paul."

"That's all right, Madame Marchand," I said. "I'll go and talk to the boys, if you don't mind."

As Uncle Maurice went inside the farmhouse with Madame Marchand, I headed for the barn.

Although Denis and Jean were supposed to be stacking the bales of hay, as I got nearer I could see they were mostly playing about, pushing and shoving one another in a play fight, and rolling all over the hay.

Antoine jumped down from a stack of hay bales and came to greet me.

"Paul!" he said. Although there was a smile of welcome on his face there was something about his expression that seemed false.

"Are you all right?" I asked.

"Yes," replied Antoine immediately, but it was too automatic to be real. There was a pause, then he looked around to make sure his brothers were out of earshot. Even though Denis and Jean seemed completely engrossed in their game, he wasn't satisfied.

"Let's take a walk," he said.

I followed Antoine to the gate that looked out on to their big field. I was wondering what could be wrong.

We reached the gate and Antoine leaned against the top bar and looked out over the field.

"Well?" I prompted. "What is it?"

"I think my father's up to something," he said.

My heart leapt when I heard him say this. Had Antoine found out about his father being in the Resistance?

"What do you mean?" I asked.

"I'm sure he's involved in something," said Antoine.

"I can tell by the way he does things. Hiding things when any of us come into the room. Saying he's going off to meet certain people, and then not going there, but going somewhere else instead."

"How do you know?" I asked.

"I just know," he said curtly.

I forced a chuckle. "I'm sure you're wrong," I said. "Can you imagine your father getting up to anything he shouldn't? That'd be like my Uncle Maurice doing that! Fat chance!"

And then Antoine turned and looked at me, and my heart really sank. I could tell from the expression on his face that something in my tone of voice had alerted him to the fact that I knew something about his father. Something secretive.

"Why did you laugh like that?" he demanded.

"Like what?" I asked.

"You just laughed the way you used to when we were at school and Monsieur Armignac accused you of doing something wrong, and you had, but you pretended you hadn't. You used to do that silly laugh, like you did just now."

"Rubbish!" I retorted. "It's just a laugh, like anyone else's."

"No it isn't," said Antoine. "Remember, Paul, we've known each other since we were tiny kids. You only ever used to do that silly laugh when you were lying about something. That's why the teachers always knew it was you, because they knew about your silly laugh too."

I shook my head. "I haven't the faintest idea what you're talking about," I said stiffly.

"Yes you do!" said Antoine angrily. And he pointed his finger accusingly at me. "You know what it is, don't you? You know about my father!"

"Me?" I questioned. "Why should I know anything?"

Even as I said it, I knew the tone of my voice was all wrong.

Antoine looked at me, and his face was white with anger.

"I thought we were friends," he said.

"We are," I insisted.

"Then why are you hiding something from me?" he demanded.

"Who says I'm hiding anything?" I replied, trying to appear as angry as him. "Who says there's anything to hide?"

Antoine didn't change his expression, he just glared angrily at me. Then he said in a low voice: "When we saw Emile and his family put on that train, and that woman shot, we said we'd keep it a secret."

"And we have," I said. "I've never told anyone anything about that."

"Neither have I," said Antoine. "But it was our special secret because we were friends. Now you're hiding something from me. I can tell. Why?"

I just looked back at him and shrugged, helplessly.

"Antoine—" I began.

"Is my father a collaborator?" he demanded, spitting out the last word bitterly.

I stared at him, truly stunned.

"No!" I said. "Absolutely not! Whoever says that—"

"I say it," he retorted angrily. "For over three years our country has been under the heel of the Germans. Elsewhere across the country French men and women are fighting to get rid of them. But what has my father done? The same as your uncle – nothing. They just lie down and let the Germans walk all over them. They go up to the big house and have tea with that German-lover, Monsieur Limond."

As he said "Monsieur Limond" his voice took on a sneer.

"I'm sure that Monsieur Limond isn't really a German-lover," I said, though I could tell from the sound of my own words how hollow and awkward they sounded. Hadn't I said exactly the same things as Antoine about Monsieur Limond in earlier times?

"Oh no?" retorted Antoine. "Then why does he let the Germans in to his house for slap-up meals? How come he and his gardener, Joseph, have licences for their shotguns when the Germans won't let any true Frenchman have one."

"Maybe he only let Commandant Fleischer in for tea so he could find out what the Germans were up to," I said.

Antoine looked at me suspiciously. "Why are you standing up for Monsieur Limond all of a sudden? You always said he was a traitor to France."

I shuffled awkwardly as he glared at me. I really wasn't enjoying this.

"Maybe I was wrong," I said. "Different people are patriotic in their own ways."

"Inviting a German Commandant in for tea doesn't seem very patriotic to me," Antoine said furiously. Then he added, pointedly: "Anyway, you still haven't told me what's going on."

"I don't know what's going on!" I burst back at him angrily. "Now leave me alone!"

It really hurt me to see the look of pain on Antoine's face as I shouted at him. I wanted to say to him, "Don't be so angry. Your father is a hero. Monsieur Limond is a hero. They are all heroes, working for France." But I couldn't.

This time, when Antoine looked at me, I was sure I could see tears in his eyes, but his voice kept firm as he said: "There's something going on with my father, and I intend to find out what it is. And if I find out he's been collaborating with the Germans, I shall hate him for ever."

With that, Antoine gave me one final glare, then turned on his heel and walked away from me to the barn where his brothers were playing. I felt terrible.

After he had gone I hung about in the yard, leaning on the fence and watching the cows in the field, and every now and then looking towards the barn where Denis and Jean were still playing happily, and Antoine had gone back to work stacking the bales of hay, and ignoring me. I so much wanted to go over and tell him the truth and make everything all right between us, but I couldn't. There was too much at stake. So instead I just hung around until Uncle Maurice came out after talking to Monsieur Marchand.

As Uncle Maurice and I drove back to Chinon, I told him what Antoine had said, and how angry he'd been.

"Monsieur Marchand should tell Antoine the truth," I said.

"He doesn't want to," said Uncle Maurice. "He doesn't want to get his sons involved. He thinks it's too dangerous for them."

"But Antoine thinks his father is collaborating with the Germans," I said.

"Then that's a good disguise for anyone to have," responded Uncle Maurice. "So long as Antoine is spreading that tale around, then the Germans won't trouble his father."

"But it's so unfair!" I protested.

"What is?" asked Uncle Maurice.

"For Antoine to think that about his father."

"You thought that about me," said Uncle Maurice.

Immediately I felt guilty – Uncle Maurice was right – but aloud I protested loudly.

"All right, you may not have thought I was a collaborator, but you thought I was too friendly towards the Germans. You thought I was siding with them."

I hung my head.

"Yes," I said quietly. "I'm sorry."

Uncle Maurice laughed.

"I'm not asking you to apologize," he said. "I'm just making the point that it will turn out all right between Antoine and his father. Like it did between us."

"But that was only because you let me in to your group," I pointed out. "Why can't Monsieur Marchand do the same with Antoine? After all, Antoine's the same age as me."

"If Jacques Marchand wants his sons kept out of this business because he thinks it's safer for them, then that's the way it has to be," said Uncle Maurice.

I fell silent. Uncle Maurice was right. If Monsieur Marchand didn't want to tell Antoine, then there was nothing I could do about it, except keep quiet, and let Antoine go on hating his father for no reason. And now he hated me into the bargain.

Two weeks later I was hauling sacks of flour from the storeroom into the bakery, when Uncle Maurice came in from the tap outside, wiping his hands on a cloth.

"Right, young Paul," he said. "We have some orders to arrange, and I need your help."

My mother, who was just inside the shop, pricked up her ears at this and came into the bakery.

"What sort of orders?" she asked.

"That cousin of Monsieur Limond's is planning to send some of our cakes to her friends in Paris, providing I can get hold of the sugar I need for them," he said.

"What?" exclaimed my mother. "Paris?!"

Uncle Maurice nodded. "It seems she was really impressed by the selection you made up last time, Angeline, and she's going to be placing an order."

"But why do you need to take Paul with you?" asked my mother, puzzled. "If it's just taking an order for cakes, then perhaps I could go with you."

Uncle Maurice sighed. Ever since we'd made our delivery of the cakes, my mother had been itching to go to

Monsieur Limond's to catch a glimpse of his cousin, so she had something to add to the gossip in the town. What she looked like, what sort of clothes she wore.

"You are needed here, Angeline, to look after the shop," Uncle Maurice said. "As for Paul, I think he needs to take on more responsibility. If he's going to become a baker and take over this shop one day, he needs to know how everything is done. Not just the right mix of flour and water and salt for different types of flour, but what sort of things customers want and how to deal with customers."

My mother looked at me, a frown on her face.

"Are you sure that Paul wants to become a baker?" she asked, doubtfully.

"Oh yes, Mother," I said, nodding my head.

My mother looked at me suspiciously as if she was going to ask some more questions, but then Uncle Maurice cut in with: "Come on, we can't hang around. That's one of the important lessons he's got to learn in business: don't keep your customers waiting."

"But the boy can't go looking like he does," protested my mother. "He's covered in flour. Look at it all in his hair!"

"That's because he's a baker's apprentice," said my uncle tersely. "Be thankful he's not a pig-farmer's assistant working in slurry, think what he'd have in his hair then."

Uncle Maurice let my mother run a brush through my

hair, to get most of the flour out of it, and then we set off in his car for Monsieur Limond's house.

"What's happened?" I asked.

"It seems the parcel Monsieur Limond's cousin has been waiting for has arrived," said Uncle Maurice. "We have to arrange for it to be passed on."

Even here, with just me and him alone in his car, Uncle Maurice was being careful and not saying anything that might give away what we were doing.

"So are we going to see the –" I nearly said "British agent", but in time I stopped myself and said, "Monsieur Limond's cousin?"

Uncle Maurice shrugged.

"I hope so," he said. "Otherwise we'll have wasted a lot of time without getting an order for cakes. And your mother will be very disappointed."

As we drove along the tree-lined drive to Monsieur Limond's house, I couldn't help but look at every building and outbuilding and wonder where the German General would be hiding. Who was he? What would he look like? Was he a general in the Army, like Commandant Fleischer, or was he a member of the SS, like Commandant Geutler? I hoped he wouldn't be like Geutler. I couldn't imagine helping someone as evil and cruel as that, even if it did mean there might be peace.

I wondered if Monsieur Marchand would be there, and if so, would Antoine have followed him on his bicycle, trying to find out what his father was up to? I hoped not. I hadn't seen anything of Antoine since our argument at his father's farm. He was obviously too angry to come and make up with me, and I was worried about saying something to him that might give away the secret about the Resistance, so I had avoided going to see him. I mentioned to Uncle Maurice my fear that Antoine might follow his father to Monsieur Limond's.

"We don't know if Monsieur Marchand is going to be there," he said, "but if he is, and Antoine has followed him, Joseph will take care of him. Joseph is used to dealing with people who sneak around the estate, that's why Monsieur Limond never has any trouble with poachers. And with all that's going on, Joseph is being extra watchful."

At Monsieur Limond's house, Uncle Maurice knocked and then rang the bell, but there was no answer.

"Perhaps they're out," I suggested.

Uncle Maurice shook his head. "The message was to come along. They'll be here," he said. "I expect they just think we'll walk in."

He pushed open the door and we entered the room. We had barely stepped inside, when a hand grabbed me roughly at the back of the neck and threw me face first against a wall. I felt Uncle Maurice crash against me. My first thought was, "Germans! We've been caught!" Then a voice barked out in French, "So, the baker and his boy! Bring them in!"

I turned and saw two men, one tall and bald, the other small with long dark hair. Both were wearing ordinary working-men's clothes. One held a rifle, the other was holding a sub-machine gun. I didn't recognize either of them.

"In the kitchen!" snapped the taller man, jabbing at us with the barrel of his rifle. "And keep your hands where I can see them!"

I followed Uncle Maurice into the kitchen, bewildered. What was going on? Who were these men?

The man with the rifle followed us into the kitchen, leaving the one with the sub-machine gun in the hallway outside to keep guard.

Monsieur Limond was in the kitchen, sitting on a hard-backed chair, with a third man standing beside him. This man had a big moustache. He also had a rifle. There was no sign of Françoise.

"Good," grunted the moustached man. "Maybe we'll get some more sense out of these two."

"They know nothing," said Monsieur Limond. "They're just a couple of men from the town."

The man with the moustache laughed.

"Really, Monsieur Limond," he chuckled. "Do you take us for idiots? In the Maquis we need to know who is on our side and who isn't, and some of our friends in the

Resistance who feel we ought to work together more closely keep us well informed."

"Too well informed, if you ask me," said Monsieur Limond sourly. "The more people who know names, the more chance there is of French patriots being shot because of loose talk."

"No one will be shot because of the Maquis," retorted the moustached man angrily. "We know how vital it is to keep silent."

"You won't keep silent under torture if the SS get hold of you," said Uncle Maurice.

"We won't get caught," said the bald man with the rifle. "We'll die first."

So these men were from the Maquis. Until they had shot Sergeant Boulet, I'd admired them and what they were doing for France – I had wanted to be like them. Since they'd killed the Sergeant, and caused 20 men from Chinon to be executed, I had changed my mind. There was no doubt they were brave, and that they were patriots, but I now agreed with Uncle Maurice: they were dangerous. And not just to the Germans, but to the French, too.

"Carry on searching the buildings," the man with the moustache said to the other two. "Outhouses. Cellars. Lofts. Everywhere. They must be here somewhere."

The man nodded and went out. Then the moustached man turned to me and Uncle Maurice.

"I'll come straight to the point," said the moustached man. "Since Monsieur Limond refuses to tell me anything, I hope that you two, as patriots wanting to free France, will. We want to know where the German is."

Uncle Maurice frowned.

"What German?" he asked.

"General Wexel," answered the man. "Well, boy?" he demanded of me.

I shrugged my shoulders.

"I've never even heard of General Wexel," I said, looking him firmly straight in the eye.

It was true, although I did my best to stop my heart from beating too hard. So that was the name of the high-ranking German officer the British agent had told us was coming.

The man with the moustache nodded, and said to us: "All right, perhaps you may not know his name. But our information is that a British agent, whom your cell have helped to get in and out of France, is planning to smuggle General Wexel to England sometime soon."

"What if we are?" demanded Monsieur Limond. "What is that to do with the Maquis?"

"French people should not be helping Germans escape," snapped the man. "We can use the information he has to help France. Afterwards, the British and the French can have him."

"If there is anything left of him," grunted Monsieur Limond.

"That is not your concern," snapped the man. "Our only aim is to free France from the Germans."

"If you know so much, then you know that this German General may be able to achieve that for us, and with fewer French people dying. If we can get a peace negotiated…"

The man with the moustache laughed, a harsh bitter laugh.

"Do you really believe that?" he demanded. "For all you know, this General is going give the British false information which will lead to a victory for the Germans."

"I trust my contact," said Monsieur Limond firmly. "I trust what the British say."

The man spat on the floor, contemptuously.

"The British have their own agenda," he snapped angrily. "They will betray us in a moment if it suits their purpose."

"How would betraying us help the British?" I asked.

The man with the moustache turned to me.

"So, the little one speaks," he said. "Who knows why politicians do the things they do? The British don't want our own Resistance leaders to take over when this war has ended. They have their own candidates in mind. They will make deals with anyone to ensure the government they want. Well we've had enough of false governments with this Vichy crowd of traitors."

"The main thing is to end the War and defeat the Germans," I said.

The man looked at Monsieur Limond and at my Uncle Maurice.

"The boy has courage," he said. "Most boys, when faced with a man with a gun, wouldn't argue with him."

"Of course he has courage," said Uncle Maurice. "And he doesn't have to prove it by shooting down French citizens."

The man with the moustache reacted angrily at this.

"If you're talking about that sergeant of yours…" he began, hotly.

"Yes, I am," snapped back Uncle Maurice. "He was just a Frenchman doing his job."

"Working for the Germans," sneered the man. "He was a collaborator. He deserved to die."

"He was no collaborator!" I interrupted. "He looked after me when I was in jail."

"How do you know who's a collaborator and who isn't, young man?" demanded the moustached man. "For all you know, this British agent of yours could well be a double-agent, playing tricks on you. It wouldn't be the first time it's happened, an agent being turned under torture. Maybe it's all part of a plot to find out who you all are before they round you up."

I was about to give an angry retort to his, but Uncle Maurice gave me a look that told me to shut up.

The two men came back into the room, and the dark-haired one said to the man with the moustache: "We'd better go. We've been here too long already."

"Any sign?" asked the man with the moustache.

The other two men shook their heads.

The man with the moustache turned back to Monsieur Limond.

"This isn't the last you've heard," he said. "We want General Wexel, and we're going to take him from you. And if any of you try and get in our way, then we'll kill you as collaborators for helping a German escape. You've been warned."

With that, the three men left.

Uncle Maurice looked at Monsieur Limond.

"We have a problem," he said.

"We do indeed," replied Monsieur Limond.

He walked to the window and watched the three men get into a battered old truck that had been parked out of sight behind a wall. Once he was sure they were gone, he walked over to the wall by the hearth of the large fireplace, took hold of a an iron hook poking out of the stonework, pushed it down, and then began to pull at it. To my astonishment, part of the wall next to the fireplace opened like a door, and the woman I knew as Françoise came out from her hiding place into the room. Behind her came a shortish man with close-cropped hair, dressed in workmen's clothes, and behind him followed Joseph.

Monsieur Limond pushed the stone-covered "door" back into place again, and the wall looked as innocent as before.

"That secret door leads down to a cellar below the kitchen," Monsieur Limond explained, seeing my mouth wide open in amazement. "I think it was used during the Revolution for hiding aristocrats who were fleeing the mob."

"It's certainly useful now," said Françoise.

"Did you hear the conversation?" Monsieur Limond asked.

She nodded. "We kept our ears to the grille in the hearth and heard every word," she said.

I was looking at the strange man, and he must have caught the suspicious look in my eye, because he gave a brief bow of his head, and said, "I thank you, gentlemen."

Although he spoke in French, there was no mistaking his German accent.

Françoise shrugged, and said, "It is only right that you meet the man you are helping, and who will hopefully help us to bring this war to a speedy end."

My heart leapt. So this was General Wexel!

I was in a turmoil. I didn't know whether to greet him as an ally, or to hit him as an enemy. I hated the Germans and everything they stood for, and here I was in the same room as one of their generals, helping him to get away.

Despite what Françoise had told us, as I looked at the General I couldn't help but sympathize with what the man from the Maquis had said: French people should not be helping Germans escape. But that's what I was doing – for the good of France.

The General looked at me, and then said to Françoise, "Your young man doesn't like me."

"His father was killed by Germans three years ago, when your country invaded ours," said Uncle Maurice.

General Wexel bowed his head towards me.

"I am sorry," he said. "My two sons were killed last year fighting the British in North Africa. They died bravely, but it still hurts to lose someone."

"Perhaps if the General will excuse us," said Françoise. "This business of the Maquis suddenly appearing will mean a slight change of plans. We have things to discuss."

"Of course," nodded the General. "I will go to my hiding place."

Instead of going to the stone door by the hearth and opening it, as I expected, the General headed for the back door, followed by Joseph. I saw Joseph look out carefully, making sure that no one was about, and then he gestured to the General and they both left the house.

"There are many places on this estate where someone can hide," Monsieur Limond explained. "The General and I prefer him to be somewhere away from the house. If he is caught by a surprise search, it makes explanations a little easier for me. I can at least try to claim that I didn't know he was even on my estate."

I looked at the closed door through which the General had gone. Despite what he had said about his two sons being killed by the British, I couldn't feel sorry for him. The Germans had started the War. Any deaths they suffered they had brought on themselves. My father and the woman at the railway station, and the 20 men who'd died in the town square, hadn't asked for a war.

The others were talking.

"What are we going to do?" asked Uncle Maurice. "The Maquis will be watching, and they will try and get hold of the General."

"So will the Germans," said Françoise.

Monsieur Limond spoke to her. "I haven't had time to tell our friends here your latest information." Turning to us, he said, "The Germans have realized that General Wexel has disappeared."

"The General was supposed to be at home on leave," added Françoise. "When they found he wasn't at his house, they got suspicious. The SS are now looking for him, and they're looking everywhere. And that includes here, in the Loire Valley."

"Perhaps they just think he might have been killed," I suggested.

Françoise shook her head.

"According to my information, Wexel is one of many generals who the SS are suspicious of. They think that some of them might be ready to surrender."

"Why?" I asked.

"Because the War is going badly for the Germans," she said. "Italy has just surrendered to the Allies. The Germans are now fighting the War on their own, and since the Americans came in on the side of the Allies, things aren't looking good for them. Earlier this year they lost the whole of Rommel's army in North Africa. That was a major blow for them."

Her words made me feel like shouting out with joy.

"So what they've been saying on the radio is right, the Germans are losing the War!" I said. "We are going to beat them!"

"We hope so," said Françoise. "But we still have a long way to go. Which is why getting General Wexel to England is so important."

"But how?" asked Uncle Maurice. "We know the Maquis are going to try to stop us, now you say the Germans may looking for him here as well."

Françoise nodded. "We're going to need a diversion," she said. "Certainly to keep the Maquis off our backs."

"What sort of diversion?" asked Monsieur Limond.

"I don't know," she said. And then she began to pace backwards and forwards across the floor, a frown of concentration on her face.

"Two planes from England," she said. I could see that she was thinking the plan through as she spoke about it. "The first comes in towards a field outside town. That's the one the Maquis think is the plane coming to collect General Wexel. That's the one they go for. Meanwhile, another plane comes in five minutes later and lands in a field nearer here. That's the one the General and I get on, and fly back to England."

"How do you know the Maquis will be fooled by the first plane?" asked Monsieur Limond.

"Because we help them to think it," said Françoise. "Maybe a word from someone who thinks that what the Maquis is doing is the right way?" And she gave me a smile. "What do you think, Pierre?"

"No!" snapped Uncle Maurice. "It's too dangerous. What happens when they find out he lied to them? You heard what they said. If anyone gets in their way, or helps the General escape, they'll kill them."

"The Maquis won't know that our young friend here has lied," insisted François. "All he has to do is make them think he believes in them, and he believes that the first plane is the real plane. They'll blame us, not him."

"No!" repeated my uncle again, even more firmly.

"I'll do it," I said.

My uncle turned to me, his face angry.

"You mustn't!" he said.

"I must," I replied firmly. "Mademoiselle Françoise is right, I'm the only one they'll believe."

"It might work even better if some of us actually went to

the decoy dropping point to wait for the plane," Monsieur Limond said to Uncle Maurice. "You and Monsieur Pommeline, for example, along with young … Pierre, here. You could go through the usual procedures as if you were expecting the plane to land, and when the Maquis turn up and try to take over, you start protesting. Then, when the plane doesn't actually land, but just flies on, you can all be surprised."

"But what about the fact that the General won't be there with us?" demanded Uncle Maurice, still not convinced.

"You say that you're expecting him to arrive, brought by the British agent," replied Monsieur Limond. "When they don't turn up, you tell them that something must have happened at the last minute causing a change in plan. After all, this is supposed to be secret. Things are always changing at a moment's notice."

"I don't like it," said Uncle Maurice unhappily. "For one thing, how is Pierre supposed to find these thugs from the Maquis?"

"He won't need to," said Françoise. "Remember, they said they'll be watching you. Believe me, the Maquis are not the most patient of people. I'm pretty sure they'll make contact with our young friend here and start asking him questions. All he has to do is give the answers we want them to have."

"I can do that," I said.

"So, when is it to be?" asked Monsieur Limond.

"Let's say a week's time," said Françoise. "That'll give me time to get in touch with London, and also for the Maquis to get in touch with young Pierre."

Monsieur Limond shook his head. "A week's too long," he said. "The SS are sniffing around. They could come here searching any day and find the General. Every day he's hidden here adds to the risk."

Françoise shrugged.

"I could get in touch with London and make the pick-up sooner, but what about the Maquis?"

"I won't wait for them to get in touch with me, I'll get in touch with them," I said.

Uncle Maurice looked gloomy at this. He didn't want me to be so deeply involved, but he knew the success of the plan depended on it.

"Do you think you can do it in the next two days?" asked Françoise.

I nodded.

"If they're going to be watching us, I'm sure I can," I said.

"In that case, I'll see if I can arrange the pick-up for three days' time," she replied.

Uncle Maurice was silent for most of the drive home. I could tell by the expression on his face that he was very unhappy about what I was going to do. Finally, he blurted out: "I wish I'd never brought you into this business!"

"I'm glad you did," I said. Then I asked the question that had been on my mind ever since the Maquis had left.

"Do you think the Maquis may be right?" I asked, warily. "Say this General is a double-agent taking false information to England?"

Uncle Maurice let out a deep sigh.

"In this war, who can tell who's telling the truth and who isn't?" he asked. "Still, if I were you, I'd keep asking yourself that question. It might help you seem convincing when you pretend to betray us to the Maquis."

"How am I going to do that?" I asked. "Betray you, I mean?"

Uncle Maurice grinned slightly.

"You were very confident at Monsieur Limond's house when you were talking to Ma'mselle Françoise," he smiled.

"I am confident," I said. "I'm just not sure how to do it exactly."

"The simplest way is always the best," said Uncle Maurice. "The more complicated it is, the more things there are to go wrong."

"So what's the simple way?" I asked.

"We're agreed the Maquis will be watching us?" he said.

I nodded.

"My guess is that it'll be one of those three men we met at Monsieur Limond's who'll be keeping an eye on us. You go up to whichever one of them's watching and say you agree with him and you want to give him details of when and where we're smuggling the German General out of France. He'll ask for the details, and you say you don't know them yet, but you'll try and find out when. Say you won't know where the pick-up will be done until the actual night, so they'll have to follow us. Have you got that so far?"

I nodded again.

"Tell him you'll write the time and day on a tiny piece of paper, screw it up, and put it in a cake," Uncle Maurice continued. "Tell him to come into the shop and you'll give him the cake with the details inside it."

"Won't anyone notice the cake looks a bit messy if I stuff paper in it?" I asked.

"Not if it's a custard tart," said Uncle Maurice. "You can roll the paper up and push it into the custard filling, then smooth the filling over again. No one will be suspicious."

"A custard tart," I nodded. "Right."

"Just make sure you keep it away from the other custard tarts," grinned Uncle Maurice. "We don't want one of our regular customers to choke on a screwed-up piece of paper."

A couple of days later I was helping Uncle Maurice unload sacks of flour from the back of his car and take them into the bakery at the back of the shop, when I spotted the man with the moustache from the Maquis hanging around at the end of the back alley. He was keeping a watch on us as he had threatened to do. I expected that his two comrades were keeping the same sort of eye on Monsieur Limond's house, and also Monsieur Marchand's farm.

As Uncle Maurice and I carried one of the sacks in, I whispered to him: "The Maquis man is here."

"I know, I saw him," Uncle Maurice whispered back. "Are you still sure you want to do this, Paul?"

I nodded, although I had a tight feeling in my stomach. I didn't like to admit to Uncle Maurice that I felt nervous. Suppose the man didn't believe me? Suppose he got rough with me? I would be on my own with him, away from any help.

"You're really sure?" persisted Uncle Maurice.

"Yes," I said.

"Very well," said Uncle Maurice. "Get your coat and go and run an errand for me. Go to Madame Chinoux's drapery shop and ask her if she has any samples of muslin."

"Muslin?" I asked.

"It's a cloth," said Uncle Maurice. "You can wrap wet dough in it. Tell her I'm thinking of using it to shape a new sort of pastry, and I wonder how much it costs, and if she's got any examples. And, while you're doing that, you can talk to your friend at the end of the alley."

"Right," I said, and I grabbed my jacket from the peg on the back of the door.

"Be careful, Paul," my uncle warned.

"I will, Uncle," I said.

I left the bakery by the back door, and headed along the alley towards the main street. The man seemed surprised to see me coming towards him, but he didn't make any move to approach me. I suppose he was keeping his attention on Uncle Maurice and what he was up to. The nearer I got to the man, the more nervous I felt, although I did my best not to show it. Say I made that "silly laugh" that Antoine had talked about, and gave myself away. I had to keep tight control on myself and make the man believe me.

As I drew level with him, I cast a quick look back over my shoulder towards the bakery, and then whispered to the man: "Psst!" and jerked my head towards a yard at the back of what used to be the undertaker's, but now stood empty. Since the War had started, the undertaker had moved into a much bigger place.

The Maquis man looked all around him before joining me in the yard.

"What?" he demanded.

"My uncle has sent me out on an errand. We have to be quick or he'll get suspicious and wonder what I'm up to."

"Why would he be suspicious?"

"If he saw me talking to you."

"Why?"

"Because … because he knows I don't always agree with the way he does things. With the Resistance, I mean. I think we're too soft on the Germans!"

The man smiled broadly.

"I knew you were one of us!" he said. "You're not frightened of proper fighting, are you?"

"That depends who gets hurt," I said.

"Only Germans and those traitors who help them," he said curtly.

"Do you really think this German General might be a double-agent?" I asked.

"Of course," answered the man. "These Germans don't give themselves up that easily. Why?"

I hesitated, and lowered my voice to a whisper. "Because I'm supposed to help him get away," I said.

The man's face showed his eagerness. "Where? When?" he demanded urgently.

"I don't want any of our people hurt," I said defiantly. "My uncle, or any of the others. They're doing their patriotic duty for France."

"All right, all right," growled the man. "Just tell me where and when."

"I don't know yet," I explained. "I'll know tomorrow. Maybe the day after."

"Can't you ask your uncle?" demanded the man. "I need time to make our arrangements."

"If I started asking questions, it would make him suspicious," I said, keeping my cool. "Come into the shop tomorrow afternoon. If I've got the day and time when it's going to happen, I'll slip it to you on a scrap of paper hidden inside a custard tart. As to where, your best bet is to follow me on the night it happens. It'll be in one of the fields outside town. I won't know which one until we get there. I expect I'll be going there with my uncle. With luck, I'll know more tomorrow."

"Very well," he said. "It'll have to do. But I'll send one of the other men. I don't want to create suspicion by being seen hanging around Chinon too much. You can never be too careful." Then he gave a grin and slapped me on the shoulder. "Vive la France!" he said.

I left him and hurried on to Madame Chinoux's drapery shop, which was four streets away. As I walked, my legs felt weak and I could feel my heart thumping hard as if it was going to burst. I had done it, and I hadn't betrayed myself with a silly laugh. I had fooled him!

When I returned to the bakery, I had some samples of muslin from Madame Chinoux with their different prices pinned to them, and the story about my conversation with the man. Uncle Maurice listened, then nodded.

"Right," he said. "I'll go to Monsieur Limond's and see if there's any news."

"Shall I come with you?" I asked.

"No," said Uncle Maurice. "The Maquis will still be watching. It might look suspicious if we go together to Monsieur Limond's so soon after you spoke to this man."

That afternoon Uncle Maurice left me and my mother in charge of the shop while he went off to see Monsieur Limond. When he came back he muttered the words that filled me with both excitement, and fear.

"Tomorrow night," he said. "Eleven o'clock."

So soon!

That evening Uncle Maurice decided the large mixing machine in which we made up the dough needed servicing. I offered to help him, but he told me to take some rest, he could do it. Actually I think he was quite glad of the excuse to spend some time on his own. Uncle Maurice had always been a man who preferred his own company, and I suppose – especially since I'd become involved in the Resistance – he was spending more time in other people's company than he would have liked. So that evening, while Uncle Maurice worked on the dough mixer, I sat with my mother in our rooms and read a book, while she knitted a scarf that she was planning to give a friend of hers as a Christmas present.

We sat together for a while, me reading, her knitting, when suddenly she said, "Paul?"

I looked up from my book and saw she was staring at me, but for once she didn't have her usual worried expression. In fact she almost seemed to be smiling, something I hadn't seen her do since she heard the news that my father had been killed.

"Yes, Mother?" I said.

"I just want to say how happy I am that you seem to have got your life sorted out these last few months," she said. "I know these are difficult times, with the War, and the Germans occupying the country, but when that business of Monsieur Armignac happened –" and she shook her head sadly at the memory, "I really was at my wits' end. I didn't know what was going to happen to you. I had horrible visions of you getting into trouble with the Germans, and being taken away."

"That's all in the past now, Mother," I said.

"I know," she said. "And for that we both have to thank your Uncle Maurice. He is a good man, Paul. I know that you never really got on with him because he is so different from your father—"

"Uncle Maurice is all right," I cut in. "He doesn't talk so much and he isn't as friendly to people, but he is a very good man, and I trust him completely. I would never want to do anything to make him sad, or feel that I have let him down."

"I am so glad to hear you say that," said my mother.

With that she gave a big happy smile and returned to her knitting. I went back to reading my book. Inside, I knew she thought that because I was spending all my time with Uncle Maurice, my life was much steadier and safer than before. If only she knew the truth, that I was in more danger than ever.

The next day Uncle Maurice had to go out making deliveries, and once more my mother and I were left in charge of the shop. As the hours ticked by I kept watching the door, waiting for one of the men from the Maquis to come in, as I'd arranged. Every time the shop bell rang as the door opened, my heart gave a jump. But time and time again it was just one of our regular customers, come to buy bread, or cakes, or biscuits.

It was the middle of the afternoon when the stranger arrived. This time it was the tall bald man. I looked at him as he came in to the shop, and I nodded slightly, to let him know I knew why he was there. He took his place in the queue, behind two other people, Monsieur Vermond and Madame Eglantine. I reached into my pocket and took out the scrap of paper on which I'd already written the date and time the decoy plane was due to arrive: "Eleven o'clock tomorrow night. Wednesday." I screwed the paper up tightly until it was the size of a tiny pellet, pushed it into the custard of a small tart and put it to one side, so it wouldn't get mixed up with the others.

Even though there was only a small display of cakes and pastries, about a dozen in all, Madame Eglantine was taking her time making up her mind what she was going to have, as if she was choosing from a thousand different sorts.

"I'll have a lemon slice," she told my mother. Then, as my mother reached for them, she said, "No, I've changed my mind, I think I'll have a custard tart."

As my mother picked a custard tart from the tray and put

it in a bag, Madame Eglantine said, "Wait, I wonder if I ought to have a raisin cake instead. I think sometimes the custard gives me wind."

I groaned inwardly, and the bald man behind Madame Eglantine shuffled impatiently.

"No," said Madame Eglantine firmly. "I'll have the custard tart."

I heaved a sigh of relief that she had finally made up her mind, but then my heart leapt into my mouth as the door of the shop opened and a German Army officer strode in. Four armed German soldiers stayed outside.

"Papers!" snapped the German officer curtly.

Madame Eglantine and Monsieur Vermond immediately began to take out their identity papers: Madame Eglantine from her handbag and Monsieur Vermond from the inside pocket of his jacket.

"I'll just go and get ours, they're upstairs in my bag," said my mother, and she started to head towards the stairs up to our rooms.

"No need," said the German officer. "I only need to see those of your customers."

He checked Monsieur Vermond's and Madame Eglantine's papers, and then gave them back to them.

The bald man had taken his papers out, and the German officer took them from him, and scanned them. Then he looked at the bald man.

"These papers say you're from Nantes," he said.

"Yes," nodded the bald man.

"What are you doing in Chinon?" demanded the German.

"I'm looking for work," said the bald man. "The factory I used to work at in Nantes was bombed. Since then, there's been no work at Nantes. None that's safe, anyway."

The German nodded, and then, instead of giving the man his papers back, he put them in his tunic and said, "You're coming with us."

The bald man looked shocked – and worried.

"Why?" he asked.

"Routine enquiries," replied the German officer. "We check on all strangers."

"But I've done nothing wrong," protested the bald man.

"Then you have nothing to worry about," said the German officer.

He called out something in German, and two soldiers from the patrol outside came into the shop. Although he was speaking in German, it was obvious he was telling them to take the stranger away. My heart was pounding so hard I thought it would burst. Once they got the Maquis man to SS Headquarters and started questioning him, I was sure they'd get suspicious; and then the real interrogation would begin, under torture. I was sure this man would tell them everything: about me and my uncle, about everyone else, about the British agent. We were all as good as dead. And they'd interrogate us as well to find out what we knew. They'd torture us to make us name names. And then they'd kill us.

It suddenly struck me that the custard tart with my message hidden inside looked very suspicious, sitting there all on its own. There was no chance of the Maquis man getting it now, so I picked it up and put it on the tray with the other half-dozen custard tarts. I'd get rid of it after the Germans had gone.

I watched, terrified, as the soldiers marched the Maquis man out of the shop. Madame Eglantine and Monsieur Vermond and my mother also looked frightened, but not for the same reasons as me.

Please God, let something happen, I prayed silently. Let the officer say it's all a mistake and let him go!

As they squeezed to get out through the narrow shop doorway, the Maquis man went into action. He suddenly kicked out at the soldier nearest to him, and as the soldier reeled back, he grabbed his rifle from him and fired a shot into the leg of one of the two soldiers standing outside the shop. Then he swung the wooden butt of the rifle into the face of the other soldier before running off. It all happened so quickly that everyone was stunned.

The German officer shouted something angrily at the only soldier left standing, and this soldier rushed to the door of the shop, raised his rifle, and fired a shot. I heard the sound of an answering rifle from out in the street, and the soldier ducked back into the shop, before leaping out and firing again. But the Maquis man had managed to get away.

The soldier who'd been hit with the rifle butt had fallen to the ground. Now he staggered to his feet, his hand to his face, blood from his nose pouring out between his fingers. The soldier who'd been shot in the leg was rolling in agony on the ground. The others stood about helplessly. Each man knew he was going to be in for a serious telling-off when they got back to their headquarters at the Town Hall.

The German officer turned to my mother. He looked like he was trying to get his temper under control.

"Do you know that man?" he demanded.

"No," said my mother. "I've never seen him before."

The officer turned to Madame Eglantine, Monsieur Vermond, and me.

"Any of you ever seen him before?"

We all shook our heads.

The officer scowled. Then he turned to the three soldiers who were standing and barked an order at them. I guessed he was telling them to carry the wounded soldier away, because they bent down, lifted him up and began to carry him off.

The officer looked at all of us in the shop, and said, "If any of you hear anything about that man, you will come to the Town Hall and give us that information." Then his eye fell on the trays of cakes.

"Custard tarts," he said, and his eyes lit up. "Back home in Germany, we have the best custard tarts. It will be interesting to compare the taste with yours."

And with that he began to reach his hand towards the tray of custard tarts – towards the one that contained the message! But before his hand could reach the tray, I snatched it up.

"Let me put that in a bag for you, sir!" I said.

Then, as I reached for a paper bag, I let the custard tart drop on to the floor of the shop.

"Paul!" said my mother, shocked and frightened.

"I'm so sorry!" I apologized, doing my best to look very humble.

I picked up two more custard tarts, much more carefully this time, and put them both in a paper bag and handed them to the German officer.

"I'm so sorry for my son's clumsiness, sir," said my mother. "I think what happened with that man just now – the shooting and everything – has upset him and made his hands shake."

The German officer said nothing, just gave me a look, and for one awful moment I thought, "He knows!" I expected him to order me out from behind the counter and to go with him. Instead, he just nodded to my mother, Madame Eglantine and Monsieur Vermond, and marched out of the shop, holding the paper bag with the custard tarts in it.

I spent the rest of the day worried sick for so many reasons: the first was that the message about the decoy plane hadn't been delivered, and I didn't know how I was going to pass it on to the Maquis. My second worry was that the Germans would be looking for the bald man, which meant they'd be stopping and searching cars and lorries, as well as searching all the buildings in the area, and they might find General Wexel. Then a third awful thought struck me: would the Maquis think that I'd set a trap for them? That I'd told the Germans their man would be coming in? If they thought that, they'd kill me for certain.

As soon as Uncle Maurice came back, I started to tell him what had happened to the Maquis man, but he knew already. Word had spread all over town within minutes of it happening. A wanted man was on the loose, and being chased by the Germans.

"But I never got the message to him," I whispered.

"Don't worry," he said. "We'll think of something."

But I did worry. I couldn't think of what we were going to do to solve this problem. And I was especially worried that the Maquis might think I'd betrayed them.

Whether it was all the worry over what had happened, I don't know, but that night as I lay in bed I felt an uncontrollable need to go to the toilet. Usually I tried not to go to the toilet at night, because ours – like nearly everyone's else's in the town – was in a small shed outside at the back of the house. This meant going out in the cold and dark, taking a candle or an oil lamp to be able to see where I was going. There were also mice around at night, and I didn't like the idea of them running around my feet, but I just had to go.

I went downstairs, took a candle, put it in the candleholder and lit it, and then went outside, keeping my hand around the candle to shield it from the wind. As I walked towards the toilet I thought I heard a scuffling sound. "Mice", I thought unhappily. I was just reaching out to open the toilet door, when there was a gust of wind and the candle suddenly went out. The next moment I felt a hand over my mouth, and a man's voice whispered, "Don't make a sound." It was the man with the moustache.

He took his hand away from my mouth and I turned to face him.

"I … I have to go to the toilet," I stammered. After being grabbed by him like that, it was truer than ever.

"In a moment," he said. "I've been here for hours, wondering how to get hold of you. What about the plane?"

"Eleven o'clock tomorrow night," I whispered back. "My uncle, another man and I will be doing it. The British agent will be bringing the German General along separately. I don't know where he is. My uncle and I will be leaving here at about half past ten. Follow us."

In the darkness, I saw his head nodding.

"Good," he said.

"How is your friend?" I asked, nervously. "The bald man."

"He got away," replied the man. "He'll be with us."

"It wasn't me!" I blurted out. "I didn't tell the Germans he was coming in!"

"I know," he said. "After years of this, I know when people are lying and when they're honest."

As the man was about to go, I reminded him: "Remember, you promised no harm would come to my uncle or the others."

"As long as they don't get in our way when the action starts, they have nothing to worry about," said the man.

Then, as suddenly as he had appeared, he vanished into the darkness.

I stood there outside the toilet, my heart thumping with the terror of being grabbed in the dark like that, but also relief that the message had been delivered. I hurried into the toilet, not caring if mice were there or not.

From early the next morning all everyone talked about when they came into the bakery or the shop were the Germans and their hunt for the bald man.

Monsieur Entrait, probably the biggest gossip in Chinon, was one of the first who came in to the shop.

"Have you heard what happened last night?" he asked my mother, his voice full of excitement.

"No," said my mother. "What?"

"That man the Germans were looking for, the one who was in your shop yesterday…" said Monsieur Entrait, and for a moment I felt a pain in my chest, like being struck by a lead weight, which made me stop breathing for a second. Had the Germans caught the Maquis man after all? Or had they caught the man who had grabbed me in the alley in the middle of the night? As I put the fresh bread that Uncle Maurice had just made out on trays, I listened with my heart in my mouth.

"The Germans think there's more of them."

"More of whom?"

"More of the Resistance here," said Monsieur Entrait.

"I heard it from my sister who cleans at the Town Hall, and she overheard two of the Germans talking first thing this morning. They think there's a gang from somewhere else, possibly from Nantes, who are here for a particular purpose."

"What purpose?" I asked.

Monsieur Entrait shook his head. "My sister didn't hear that much," he said. "She gets the impression the Germans don't really know themselves, but one thing she was sure of: they're scouring the whole area looking for these men, so don't be surprised if you get another visit later today. My sister thinks they're going to be searching every house in Chinon. And setting up patrols on all the roads in and out."

For the whole of the rest of that day I was in turmoil. The time seemed to drag on so slowly. On the one hand I wanted the day to go quickly so we could go and carry out our mission that night; on the other I was so terrified of what might go wrong that I never wanted night-time to arrive. The whole thing made me feel so sick that when it came to lunchtime, I couldn't eat the soup and bread that mother had made for me.

"Are you feeling all right, Paul?" she asked, concerned, as I just picked at my bread.

"Yes, I'm fine," I said. "I'm just not feeling very hungry."

"I've never known you not to eat," said my mother. Turning to Uncle Maurice, she said, "I think Paul may be sickening for something. I'm going to take him over to Doctor Morelle."

"The boy isn't ill," protested Uncle Maurice.

"You don't know that," insisted my mother. "I think he ought to at least have his temperature taken."

"He's all right!" countered Uncle Maurice impatiently.

"Then why has he lost his appetite all of a sudden?" my mother demanded.

"I expect he's just been eating too many cakes and pastries behind our backs," snorted Uncle Maurice. "It's a wonder he can eat any meals at all, with the amount he stuffs into himself during the day."

"But Maurice—" protested my mother.

"No!" interrupted Uncle Maurice firmly. "I won't have the doctor disturbed unnecessarily for a boy with a simple stomach upset, when there are people with real illnesses and injuries needing treatment. And that's an end to it."

And so it was.

In the early afternoon mother went off to see a friend of hers, and Uncle Maurice and I went into the bakery to prepare the sacks of flour and blocks of fat for the next lot of dough-making. As we worked together I could tell by the expression on his face that he was worried.

I went to the door that led into the alley at the back of the bakery, to make sure that no one was outside who could overhear. Then I went to Uncle Maurice and whispered: "It's going to be difficult tonight, with the Germans watching."

"I know," growled Uncle Maurice unhappily. "Those

damned Maquis have ruined everything by coming here. We had a good system going here in the Chinon area, which the Germans never suspected. Now, by interfering the way they have, they've brought the Germans down on us, and we can hardly move. Why couldn't they have just stayed in Nantes and left us alone?"

He sat down heavily on a pile of sacks of flour and sighed.

"There will be patrols everywhere tonight, checking all vehicles," he said gloomily. "I can't use the usual excuse about getting flour for the early morning baking, not with the Germans suspicious as they are. They'll just tell me to go home and wait till dawn."

"Maybe we can tell Mademoiselle Françoise that it might be better not to do it tonight," I suggested.

"It's too late for that," said Uncle Maurice. "The planes will be arranged. Also, with all this activity by the Germans, it's more important than ever that this General is got out of the country. Every minute he stays here increases the danger to all of us. No, it has to be tonight." He sighed heavily again, staring at the ground, deep in thought. Suddenly he looked up at me, his eyes wide. "Paul, remember what your mother said at lunchtime today?"

"About my being ill because I couldn't eat my lunch?" I said, gloomily. "To be honest, Uncle, I feel so sick with it all I'm surprised I managed to eat anything at all."

"Then that's how we'll get out!" said Uncle Maurice,

standing up, with a look of grim determination on his face. "Tonight, about quarter past ten, I want you to say you feel really ill. Your stomach. Pretend to be in real pain."

"Why?" I asked.

"Because I'll tell your mother she must have been right all along, that you are ill, and I'm going to take you to Doctor Morelle. If we run into any patrols, I'll tell them the same."

"But won't Mother find out you're lying when she talks to Doctor Morelle and finds out we never went to him?" I protested.

Uncle Maurice shook his head.

"We will go to Doctor Morelle," he said. "But after we've done what we have to do."

"But what about the fact that I'm not really ill?" I persisted. "What will Doctor Morelle say about being woken up in the middle of the night for a fake patient. He's bound to tell Mother about that."

"No he won't," said Uncle Maurice. "Doctor Morelle is part of our group. He will cover for us."

I stared at Uncle Maurice, stunned at this news.

"Doctor Morelle?" I echoed.

Uncle Maurice nodded. "How do you think we treat those Allied airmen who've been shot down and need medical help?" he asked.

Doctor Morelle! My mind was in a whirl, and I began to

wonder how many other ordinary, respectable townspeople in Chinon were part of the Resistance group.

The rest of the day passed quickly. Mother returned from her visit to her friends, and Uncle Maurice and I cleaned the mixing equipment and closed up the shop.

Mother made a meal for us, but I had to tell her I couldn't eat much. Once again, she was worried that I was getting ill, and once again Uncle Maurice told her not to be silly, that I'd be all right. Even though we were setting up our excuse for leaving the house later that night, the truth was that when I thought about what lay ahead of us, with the possibility of getting caught, I really did feel sick and couldn't stand the thought of eating anything. Uncle Maurice, on the other hand, tucked into the casserole that Mother had made with a healthy appetite, which amazed me. He really was a very brave man.

That night Mother and I went to bed at ten o'clock, as usual. Uncle Maurice said he needed to stay up to do some paperwork. At a quarter past ten, as agreed, I started groaning out loud. Mother came into my room, a dressing gown thrown over her nightdress and a worried expression on her face.

"What's the matter, Paul?" she asked.

I didn't answer, just started rolling over in my bed and clutching my stomach.

"What's going on?" growled my uncle's voice. "What's all this noise?"

I groaned and moaned, then stumbled out of bed, and promptly fell on the floor, doubled over, both hands pressed against my stomach.

"It's a terrible pain…" I groaned.

"I knew he was ill!" said my mother.

Uncle Maurice came over to me and knelt down beside me, putting his hand to my forehead.

"I think he has a temperature," he said. Turning to my mother, he said, "I think you were right after all, Angeline. He really is in pain."

"What are we going to do?" asked my mother. "What if it's appendicitis? He might need an operation!"

"Leave it to me," said Uncle Maurice, taking command. "I'll take him to Doctor Morelle's."

"Isn't it a bit late for that?" said my mother. "Perhaps you should take him to the hospital."

Uncle Maurice shook his head. "The hospital's overworked as it is," he said. "We'll get better treatment from Doctor Morelle. He won't mind being woken up. Since the War started, he's become used to it." To me, he said: "Can you get your clothes on?"

I nodded and let out a bit of a groan, just to keep up the act.

"Right," said Uncle Maurice. "Get dressed. I'll get the car started."

"Perhaps I should come with you?" said Mother, as Uncle Maurice headed for the stairs.

"No," said Uncle Maurice tersely. "With the three of us in a car, it will look like we're a family fleeing. We don't want to waste time explaining ourselves to the German patrols. You stay here and look after the house. We'll be back as soon as we can."

Fifteen minutes later, Uncle Maurice and I were in his car, driving through the streets of Chinon. As we drove, my stomach really was churning. There were so many things that could go wrong. What if we were stopped by a German patrol and turned back? Even if we made it to the field, though Uncle Maurice and I were just being the decoys, the Maquis could get angry because they thought we'd fooled them. Suppose the Germans turned up at the field? Or what if what the Maquis said was true and the German General was tricking us? Maybe he'd already told the Germans what was going to happen, and everyone would be caught tonight. Anything could happen.

We had only been driving for a few minutes when we saw a patrol of German soldiers at one side of the road in the dark. Two of them stepped directly in front of us and levelled their rifles at the car.

"Start groaning," whispered Uncle Maurice. "But don't overdo it."

Uncle Maurice pulled the car to a halt and wound down his window. I doubled up in the passenger seat beside him and began moaning, clutching my stomach.

"Where are you going?" demanded one of the soldiers.

"I'm taking my nephew to Doctor Morelle's house," said Uncle Maurice. "He's got a terrible pain. I'm worried it might be appendicitis."

"Let me see your papers," demanded the soldier.

As Uncle Maurice reached into his inside jacket pocket for his papers, another soldier said, "It's all right. It's the baker. I recognize him."

This didn't impress the first soldier, who still held out his hand. Uncle Maurice gave him our papers. The soldier scanned them, while I clutched my stomach and writhed and groaned and moaned.

"He really is in a bad way," said Uncle Maurice, the tone of his voice urgent. "Perhaps you could come with us. It might speed our way to Doctor Morelle's in case we get stopped by other patrols."

The soldier glared at Uncle Maurice. "Our job isn't to act as nursemaid to children!" he snapped.

He handed Uncle Maurice his papers back, and jerked with his thumb.

"On your way!" he said.

"Thank you, monsieur," nodded Uncle Maurice, and we headed off.

He waited until we were clear of the patrol, then he said "OK, you can stop groaning now."

We carried on driving in silence, past the road that would

lead us to Doctor Morelle's house, out to the country. I began to feel a rising sense of panic. If we were stopped now our excuse that we were going to call on Doctor Morelle would be exposed as a lie.

"Is anyone following us?" I asked Uncle Maurice.

Uncle Maurice checked in his mirror.

"Not that I can see," he said. "There's no vehicles back there, but maybe they're driving without lights."

"If they did that, the Germans would surely be suspicious," I said.

"At this moment, the Germans are suspicious of everyone and everything," replied Uncle Maurice.

So, where were the Maquis? They were supposed to be following us, but so far there was no sign of them. Suddenly I worried that they'd grown suspicious. Suppose they'd decided to follow Monsieur Limond instead? That would take them straight to the real pick-up point, and the British agent and the German General.

Uncle Maurice followed the same route as before, along country roads, then along a track, and finally we arrived at the ploughed field where I'd first helped set the guiding fires to help Françoise land.

The gate to the field was shut, so I jumped out of the car and opened it, and Uncle Maurice drove in. I was just about to shut the gate again, when I saw the shape of another car coming along the track. But as it got nearer I saw that it wasn't the Maquis, it was Monsieur Marchand's car. He waved at me as he drove into the field, then I pushed the gate shut. It suddenly struck me that perhaps all the Maquis men had been arrested. In which case, I'm sure the Germans would have got out of at least one of them about the plane coming in to this field and taking the German General away. Were the Germans watching us? The whole thing was a nightmare of not knowing.

Monsieur Marchand got out of his car and waved to Uncle Maurice. "I've got some good dry wood in the car for the fires," he said. "The paraffin's in the boot."

"Right, we'll put the wood in the holes, Paul can bring the paraffin."

As Monsieur Marchand took bundles of wood from inside the front of his car and handed some of them to Uncle Maurice, I went round the back and opened the boot. As I reached in for the can of paraffin, I was sure I saw a bundle of old cloths piled on the back seat of the car move slightly. It may have been just a trick of the moonlight, or a reflection of shadows on the glass of the rear window, but I had the feeling that someone was hiding on the back seat. Was it the Maquis, or a German?

"Paul!" whispered my uncle urgently. "Hurry up with that paraffin."

"Uncle!" I whispered back.

Something in the tone of my voice made him and

Monsieur Marchand hurry over to me. I pointed at the bundle of cloth on the back seat of the car and whispered to him, "I think there's someone under there."

"Nonsense," said Monsieur Marchand, shaking his head. "No one could have got in without me noticing."

Uncle Maurice suddenly reached out, grabbed the cloth and pulled it to one side. Antoine's frightened face looked out at us.

"Antoine!" gasped his father, shocked.

"I had to find out what you were up to," mumbled Antoine.

"You stupid idiot!" snapped Uncle Maurice. Then he turned to me and Monsieur Marchand. "We haven't got time for this now. The plane will be coming in, and we need to set the fires. Come on! We'll sort this idiot out later. Paul, stay here with Antoine and make sure he doesn't do anything stupid."

Uncle Maurice and Monsieur Marchand went running towards the centre of the field as fast as they could over the ploughed furrows, carrying the cans of paraffin. Behind me I heard Antoine scramble out of the back of the car. He asked in a bewildered voice: "What's going on?"

"What do you think?" I snapped back at him. "We're the Resistance."

"What?" he said, stunned. "My father—?"

"Yes. Now shut up. We've got work to do."

"What can I do?" asked Antoine.

"Nothing," I said. "Just stay here."

It was strange, although I was only a month older than Antoine, and had only been on one mission before, I felt so much older and more experienced than him.

"But I want to help," he begged.

"Then keep watch," I said. "Let me know if you see anything."

Antoine shook his head, still stunned.

"I can't believe that my father is in the Resistance," he said.

"I felt the same when I found out about my uncle," I said.

"What's happening tonight? Why is a plane coming in?"

I was about to tell him the truth, that we were just a decoy, then realized it was safer to tell him the cover story, just in case he let it slip out.

"We're helping smuggle a German General and a British agent to England," I said. "He wants to surrender, and he's got information about what the Germans are planning."

Antoine looked around.

"Where is this German General?" he asked. "And the British agent?"

"They're coming," I said.

"I certainly hope so," growled a voice behind me.

I turned, and saw that it was the man with the moustache from the Maquis. Behind him were the two other men, the tall bald man and the short one. They were all armed. I wondered how they had got here without us noticing them. In the faint moonlight I could see the teeth of the man with the moustache as he grinned at my surprise.

"We followed you on bicycles," he said.

Then I smelt smoke, a mixture of paraffin and wood, and realized that the fires had been lit. I heard footsteps across the earth, and turned to see Uncle Maurice and Monsieur Marchand hurrying towards us. They stopped when they saw the three armed men.

"What's going on?" demanded Monsieur Marchand.

"They're here to take the General," snarled Uncle Maurice. If I hadn't known that he knew about the plan already, I would have sworn that the bitterness in his voice was real. I realized then just how good an actor Uncle Maurice was, and how cleverly he'd fooled the Germans, and me and my mother, for all these years.

"That's right," said the leader of the group and he gestured with the barrel of his rifle at Monsieur Marchand. "And if you want to stay alive, then stay out of what's going to happen."

Antoine looked absolutely bewildered by this sudden turn of events.

"What's going on?" he demanded, looking to his father, and Uncle Maurice, and to me.

"Another boy," said the short man. "This group is made up of children and old men."

"They do a man's job," said Uncle Maurice, and hearing the way he said these words made me feel proud.

Suddenly we all heard the noise: a plane was approaching.

"Where's the British agent and the General?" asked the moustached man angrily.

"I don't know," said Uncle Maurice. "They're supposed to be here. The plane's coming, we've got the fires lit to mark the pick-up."

"Maybe there's been a change of plan," said the bald man.

It was then that we heard the sound of car engines, and the heavier sound of the engine of a lorry. Though the hedges I could see the dim glow of headlights.

"That must be them," said the short man.

"Three vehicles with headlights?" snorted the moustached man. "Those are Germans." Turning to Uncle Maurice he said, "You've been sold out!"

The plane was getting nearer all the time, coming down lower.

"The General isn't coming!" snapped the moustached man, turning to Uncle Maurice and Monsieur Marchand. "Get these boys out of here!"

"But—" began Monsieur Marchand.

"Now!" shouted the man from the Maquis, his voice urgent. "We'll hold the Germans off."

The next thing I knew, Uncle Maurice grabbed me by the

collar and pushed me into his car. Monsieur Marchand did the same with Antoine.

"There's a gap in the hedge at the other side of the field!" Uncle Maurice shouted at Monsieur Marchand. "We'll go over the fields and come out in the back lane. Follow me!"

We set off, Uncle Maurice's car bouncing and lurching over the furrows of the ploughed field. We passed the middle of the field where the fires were still burning in their holes in the earth.

Then a terrific sound filled my ears as the plane came down low and then flew over us, almost hitting the roof of the car. Then it soared up into the sky.

The car bounced up and down, and I was shaken about, being thrown against the door and even banging my head on the roof as we crashed over the furrows at speed.

Because Uncle Maurice was driving without lights, I couldn't see clearly where we were going. I could make out a hedge directly in front of us as we came to the edge of the field, but I couldn't see a gap in it. I threw my hands up in front of my face to protect myself, sure we were going to crash. There was a clunk of wood on metal as we hit a branch, and suddenly we were in the next field.

Behind us I heard the sound of gunfire and shouting.

Uncle Maurice continued driving. Now that we were in an unploughed field he was able to go faster. I turned and took a quick look out of the back window. Monsieur Marchand's car was right behind us.

We reached a gate that had been left open, and drove through into a third field. Uncle Maurice obviously knew where he was going, and it struck me that he'd had this getaway route planned, just in case he might need it one time. Like tonight.

We went through two more fields, and finally we came out on to a track, which turned on to a small road. The sound of gunfire was now far behind us.

"I think we're safe," I said.

"We're never safe," said Uncle Maurice. "Make sure you remember that."

We came to a T-junction, and at last Uncle Maurice switched his headlights on.

"We don't want to draw attention to ourselves by driving around without lights," he said.

The inside of our car was suddenly lit up as Monsieur Marchand did the same behind us, his headlights dazzling me at first. Then Uncle Maurice turned right and headed back to Chinon. I looked back, and saw Monsieur Marchand turning left, heading back to his farm.

As we reached Chinon, I could still hear the sounds of gunfire in the distance. And then, suddenly, it all went quiet.

"The shooting's stopped," I said, in a hushed voice.

"I know," said Uncle Maurice. "But that's not our

problem. Right now, we have to make our call on Doctor Morelle. And there's no need to groan when you see him. Only if we run into a German patrol. All right?"

I nodded, but despite what Uncle Maurice said about it not being our problem, I couldn't help wondering what had happened to the three men from the Maquis? And I wondered what had happened to the others: to Monsieur Limond, Joseph and André, the British agent and the German General. Had the Germans also turned up where they were? Were we safe?

We arrived at Doctor Morelle's and established our alibi, and then drove back home, where Uncle Maurice told my mother that Doctor Morelle had diagnosed my stomach pains as a severe attack of indigestion caused by eating too many cakes. I did my best to look suitably ashamed of myself, and said how sorry I was for causing so much worry for everyone. My mother was so relieved that I hadn't suffered a burst appendix, or something equally serious, that she didn't get upset with me, she just hugged me to her and told me not to eat that many cakes again. I promised her I wouldn't.

The next few days were the most frustrating of my life. Uncle Maurice said we weren't to get in touch with the rest of the group straight away, as the Germans were sure to be watching everyone's movements and we didn't want to give them any reason to suspect us. This meant that I just had to sit and wait and listen to rumour and gossip about what had happened from people who came into the shop, or those I met on the street.

The biggest story was that a group of men from the Maquis had been caught by the Germans in a field outside

Chinon. In the gunfight that followed, one of the Maquis men had been shot dead, but the others had escaped. Two Germans had also been shot dead and four wounded. The Maquis who had got away managed it by driving a car right across a field and through a hedge, according to the tracks left behind. There were also signs of fires having been lit in the field, and the Germans were sure the Maquis had been waiting for a plane to land there.

I heard Madame Eglantine telling Mother all about this in the shop the next day, and I couldn't stop myself from blurting out: "Who was the man who was shot?"

Madame Eglantine shook her head.

"No one knows," she said. "He was a stranger. Not from around here. I think someone said he came from somewhere around Nantes, which was where that other man came from. You remember, the man who was in the shop that day when the Germans tried to arrest him. The good thing is it means the Germans are pretty sure all these men were from the same group, from Nantes, so they're not looking for anyone in Chinon, thank heavens."

So one of the three men had died. I wondered which one. I found out later from Uncle Maurice, who got the information from a friend of his.

"It was the man with the big moustache who died," he told me. He shook his head sorrowfully. "He was a brave man. And he died saving our lives."

"He died because we led him into a trap," I said, feeling guilty. "I led him into a trap by giving him false information. It's my fault he's dead."

Uncle Maurice shook his head.

"No!" he said firmly. "The Germans had been following those three men, trying to find out what they were up to. I was told that they were on the trail of one of them, following him on his bicycle, but not getting too near him because they wanted him to lead them to his comrades. So the shoot-out between them and the Germans would have happened anyway. At least this way, it didn't happen at the field where the General was being picked up."

"Did the General get away?" I asked.

"I don't know," replied Uncle Maurice.

And that was as much as I knew.

During the two days after the night's shooting, the Germans increased their activity. They were determined to find the men from the Maquis who'd got away, and so they began searching everywhere in Chinon, and the farms and villages around. They even came into our bakery and started searching the sacks of flour in case people were hiding in them. They searched every shop and every house in our street, but they found nothing. They went through every outbuilding on every farm, and every derelict building. Still they found nothing. The two other men from the Maquis had vanished.

Desperate for news, I decided to ride over to the Marchand's on my bike. On my way I was stopped by a German patrol, who asked me who I was and where I was going. They even searched me, but I just played the part of an innocent helpless French boy who was unhappy at the trouble the Maquis had brought on us all, and they let me go.

Antoine was the first person I saw as I cycled into their farmyard. He ran towards me and hurried me into one of their barns. He was smiling broadly and there was an excited look in his eyes.

"Wasn't that fantastic, Paul?" he burst out. "And we did it! You and me, and my father, and your uncle!"

"And lots of other people besides," I pointed out.

"I know," Antoine nodded. "My father told me about Monsieur Limond. I feel so bad about those things I said about him."

"No need to," I assured him. "I said the same things before I found out the truth. I said worse things, in fact. Has your father had any news about the German General and the English spy?"

Antoine shook his head.

"No," he said. "He said at the moment it's best to keep radio silence while the Germans are carrying out their searches."

"Did they get away?" I asked.

"Father says he doesn't know," said Antoine. "But I

reckon they must have. If Monsieur Limond had been caught with the General by the Germans then we'd have all known about it."

"They may not have been caught, but it doesn't mean the General actually got away," I said. "They may have had to abandon the plan. He might still be in France."

"That's true," nodded Antoine. "When will we know?"

I shrugged.

"As soon as Monsieur Limond thinks it's safe for us to be told, I suppose," I said.

It was a few days later, at the start of December, that Uncle Maurice told me that we were going to take some bread rolls to Monsieur Limond.

"Is his cousin back?" I asked eagerly.

Uncle Maurice shook his head.

"No," he said. "He just wants some rolls for himself."

All the way to Monsieur Limond's I was bursting with impatience, desperate to find out what had happened that night. Had the General and the English spy got away safely?

Monsieur Marchand and Antoine were already in the kitchen with Monsieur Limond when Uncle Maurice and I walked in with our tray of rolls.

"Excellent!" smiled Monsieur Limond. "Put them on the table, Maurice. We can eat them while we have tea. Joseph and André are patrolling the grounds, so I think we are safe to talk."

As Monsieur Limond poured the tea for us, I couldn't help blurting out: "Did they get to England? Mademoiselle Françoise and ... the package she was taking?"

"Indeed they did, Paul," answered Monsieur Limond. "Thanks to your diversion, we were able to get them on board the plane that night. I've heard since that the General's information has been very useful. Françoise sends her regards to all of you, and hopes that we may all be able to meet soon, in freedom. So, let's drink a toast to that."

And he raised his cup of tea. We each picked up our cups and joined him in the toast.

"To victory. And to a free France."

It was a lot longer than we hoped before our dream of freedom was achieved. For the next nine months we remained under German rule. Although in Chinon our Resistance group maintained a low profile, in other areas the Maquis and the Resistance carried out many attacks. Curfews were in operation, which meant that no one was allowed out at night. If anyone was caught, they were in danger of being shot on sight.

It became much too dangerous for Mademoiselle Françoise to return to Chinon, especially now the Germans had discovered the fields that had been used for the drop-offs and pick-ups. All we could do was get on with our lives and try and sort out the gossip from the truth in the stories that were passed around about what was happening elsewhere in the War. That, and carry on the fight as best we could.

Antoine was eventually allowed to join our group. His father didn't want him to, but as he had been involved in that one operation, and knew the rest of the group, Monsieur Marchand gave in to the idea that it was better to have Antoine where he could see him. For me this was wonderful, it meant that I no longer had to lie to my best friend.

Together, Antoine and I sent radio messages to the British, telling them where the German troops were, and where they kept their tanks and planes hidden, so that the Allied planes could bomb them.

Because our group didn't carry out direct attacks on the Germans, they became slightly relaxed about keeping the curfew in our area. We were able to sneak out sometimes at night to get British pilots or spies to safety. There was great excitement when a British pilot was passed to us by another group. He had been shot down and we had to get him out of France. We used a different field, but we still used the same method: four holes dug in the middle, filled with sticks and paraffin. Because we were smuggling someone out, the British plane had to land on the field, just long enough for the pilot to be pulled aboard, and then the plane was off again, soaring up into the night sky.

During those nine months, Antoine and I helped four shot-down British airmen and three spies back to England. A part of me kept hoping that one day one of the planes would bring the English spy, Mademoiselle Françoise, but I never saw her again.

In June 1944 the Allies at last launched a big attack on the north coast of France and began to push the Germans back, although it was August before the big American tanks rolled into our area. The Germans had packed up their lorries and fled just days before the Americans arrived.

The days that followed their arrival were wonderful, with everyone dancing in the streets and giving the Americans presents. They gave us chewing gum, a strange sticky sweet stuff that you weren't allowed to swallow.

After the Germans had gone some of the local people had their revenge on those French people who'd supported them. Some of them were badly beaten. Most of them were arrested and sent to prison to await trial as traitors. Some of the women who'd been friendly with the Germans had their heads shaved – I saw this happen to about six women in Chinon. The most hated man in our town, Monsieur Armignac just disappeared one day, and we never saw him again. Someone said he'd fled abroad, taking money and loot the Germans had given him, which had been taken from the Jews, but no one knew where he'd gone.

Later, the Allies arrested the German leaders and put them on trial, except Hitler himself, who'd apparently committed suicide. I wondered if Commandant Geutler was among those they arrested. I hoped so.

In 1945 I finally found out what had happened to Emile and his family. The Allies went into the camps in Poland and Eastern Germany where the Jews and other people had been kept. They hadn't been labour camps at all, they had been extermination camps. Millions of Jews who had been sent there had been packed into large rooms and gassed to death.

Their bodies had then been burnt in huge ovens. It was said that ten million men, women and children had died this way. Among them had been Emile and his family. Even now, when I think of it, I feel a shadow of darkness hanging over me and I want to cry for Emile, and for his family, and for all those millions of people who were killed for no reason.

But now I try to get back to a normal life. I still work at the bakery with my Uncle Maurice. Antoine works the farm with his father. And now and then Antoine and I get together and talk about Emile, and the occupation, and the night we helped the German General get away. The time when we smuggled spies.

HISTORICAL NOTE

Soon after Germany invaded France in 1940, the French Government surrendered, and was replaced by one that promoted collaboration with Hitler. This new French Government was based at a town called Vichy, and became known as the Vichy Government. It was led by the new Head of State, Marshal Pétain. However, the real rulers of France during the Second World War were the Germans.

Hitler's main target was the Jews. He had a plan called "The Final Solution", which aimed at the extermination of the Jewish race. He had already ordered the arrest of all Jews in the other countries occupied by the Germans. These Jews were sent to extermination camps at Auschwitz, Belsen, Dachau, Buchenwald, Treblinka and other cities in German-occupied Eastern Europe. The Jews who were sent to these camps went under the impression they were being sent there to work. In fact, they were killed in gas chambers and their bodies burned. Estimates vary as to how many actually died in these camps, with figures believed to be between five million and ten million.

The removal and extermination of French Jews started

in March 1942. To ensure that these orders were carried out, German rule in France became harsher. Some non-Jewish French people protested, and they, too, were sent to the camps and killed. This led to further protest by French people, which led to harsher repression by the occupying Germans. As a result more and more people began to support and join the small groups that were fighting a guerrilla campaign within France against the occupying German troops.

From January 1943, many of these groups worked together under the name MUR (*Mouvements Unis de la Resistance*). They carried out acts of sabotage in France to hinder the German military machine. These acts included interfering with railway tracks, de-railing trains, and blowing up bridges. They also helped Allied airmen, who had been shot down over France by the Germans, to escape and they protected escaped prisoners of war. They also smuggled Jews out of France to safer countries. There was rivalry between many of the Resistance groups, between those who supported General Charles de Gaulle (considered to be France's President in exile), and those who wanted a Communist Government for France after the War.

It was the Allied invasion of France in June 1944 that really united all these separate Resistance groups, giving vital support to the Allies as they advanced across France towards Germany.

In June 1944 de Gaulle returned to France in triumph and was officially recognized as the new Head of France by Britain, the USA, the USSR and Canada. In August, as the Germans continued to retreat, de Gaulle headed a parade in Paris, from the Arc de Triomphe to Notre Dame, to massive acclaim.

In September 1944 special courts were set up throughout France to try those French people who had collaborated with the Germans during the occupation. Some of those found guilty of collaboration were executed. However, the most senior members of the Vichy Government had already been removed from France to Germany for their own safety.

On 8 May 1945 the Germans surrendered. Those members of the Vichy Government who were caught by the Allies were returned to France and tried for treason. Four of them were sentenced to death, although the sentence on Pétain was later reduced to life imprisonment.

TIMELINE

September 1939 Germany invades Poland. Great Britain, New Zealand, Australia and France declare war on Germany. USSR (Union of Soviet Socialistic Republics) invades eastern Poland. Poland divided between Germany and USSR.

February 1940 Building of concentration camp at Auschwitz begins.

April 1940 Germany invades Denmark and Norway.

May 1940 Germany invades Belgium, Holland, Luxembourg and France.

June 1940 France surrenders to Germany. De Gaulle makes speech calling for France to continue to resist the German invasion.

July 1940 New French Government (under Pétain) moves to Vichy. Pétain's Government breaks off diplomatic relations with Britain.

8 August – 15 September 1940 Battle of Britain.

September 1940 German decree requires a census of Jews.

October 1940 Vichy Government introduces first "Statut des Juifs", defining Jewishness and banning Jews from higher public service and positions influencing public opinion.

November 1940 First public demonstration against German occupation in Paris.

March 1941 Germany attacks Bulgaria.

April 1941 Germany attacks Yugoslavia and Greece. Both surrender.

June 1941 Germany attacks Russia.

July 1941 Vichy law authorizes confiscation of Jewish property and businesses.

October 1941 German Commandant of Nantes shot by the Resistance. Germans execute 27 hostages at Chateaubriant, 20 at Nantes and 50 hostages at Bordeaux.

December 1941 Japan attacks Pearl Harbor. America enters the War.

27 March 1942 First trainload of Jews leaves Drancy for Auschwitz.

June 1942 Responsibility for security in France transferred from the German Army to the SS, Hitler's Special Unit, because of activity by the Resistance.

January 1943 Milice Française founded – a French pro-German military organization set up to support the German occupation. French Resistance formed by three formerly separate groups (Combat, Liberation-Sud and Franc-Tireur) joining forces. They call themselves the MUR (Mouvements Unis de la Resistance).

April 1944 SS troops massacre 86 people at Ascq near Lille.

June 1944 D-Day landings. SS troops massacre 642 people near Limoges.

July 1944 Attempt to assassinate Hitler fails.

August 1944 French and Allied troops reach Provence. Street fighting begins in Paris. SS troops massacre 126 people at Maille, near Tours. De Gaulle heads parade from the Arc de Triomphe to Notre Dame.

January 1945 Soviet troops enter Auschwitz.

March 1945 Allies liberate Buchenwald and Belsen.

8 May 1945 Germans surrender. VE (Victory in Europe) Day.

EXPERIENCE HISTORY FIRST-HAND

HERO AT DUNKIRK

MY STORY

VINCE CROSS

BATTLE OF BRITAIN

MY STORY

CHRIS PRIESTLEY

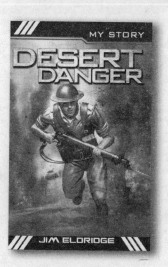

DESERT DANGER

MY STORY

JIM ELDRIDGE

WAR SPY

MY STORY

JIM ELDRIDGE